A stranger was in his house!

Rob followed the wet footprints to the room on the right. He reached down and opened the door just as the children ran up behind him.

"Daddy, there's a lady in your bed!" Michael called out.

Rob's gaze focused on the bed, and he discovered his son was right.

"Who are you?" the woman demanded in a shaky voice as she clutched the sheet.

"Don't you think that should be my line?" Rob blustered. "This is my house!"

"Daddy," Cathy whispered as she tugged on his arm, "she's Goldilocks. She ate our macaroni, sat in our chairs and slept in your bed. Just like Goldilocks."

"Goldilocks slept in Baby Bear's bed, not Papa Bear's," Rob protested. Then he felt his body grow suddenly hot as he looked at the stranger's wide blue eyes, her creamy skin and her one bare shoulder. Bare? Oh, boy. Michael had been right. There was a woman in his bed—a *naked* woman!

Dear Reader,

Once upon a time we were little girls dreaming of handsome princes on white chargers, of fairy godmothers who'd made us into beautiful princesses, and of mountain castles where we'd live happily ever after.

Now that we're all grown up, we can recapture those dreams in a brand-new miniseries, ONCE UPON A KISS. It features stories based on some of the world's best-loved fairy tales—expressly for the little girl who still lives on inside of us.

Judy Christenberry continues the series with the retelling of the classic fairy tale "Goldilocks and the Three Bears."

Be sure to read all six of these wonderful fairy-tale romances, coming to you only from American Romance!

ONCE UPON A KISS—at the heart of every little girl's dreams...and every woman's fantasy....

Happy reading!

Debra Matteucci
Senior Editor & Editorial Coordinator
Harlequin Books
300 East 42nd Street
New York, NY 10017

Judy
Christenberry

IN PAPA
BEAR'S BED

Harlequin Books

TORONTO • NEW YORK • LONDON
AMSTERDAM • PARIS • SYDNEY • HAMBURG
STOCKHOLM • ATHENS • TOKYO • MILAN
MADRID • WARSAW • BUDAPEST • AUCKLAND

ISBN 0-373-16701-6

IN PAPA BEAR'S BED

Copyright © 1997 by Judy Russell Christenberry.

This edition published by arrangement with Harlequin Books S.A.

® and TM are trademarks of the publisher. Trademarks indicated with
® are registered in the United States Patent and Trademark Office, the
Canadian Trade Marks Office and in other countries.

Printed in U.S.A.

Chapter One

The driving snow fell, settling on the hood of her car.

Jessica Barnes couldn't believe the rain that had followed her from Kansas City had turned into a snowstorm. That was unheard of in November.

Snow. Unbelievable snow.

Shaking her head, wondering if she was in shock, Jessica finally released her seat belt. It had saved her from a possible concussion when her little Mercedes had slid off the road into the steep ditch alongside it.

She'd left Kansas City and drove south into Missouri, wanting some time to herself to think. Now it looked as if she was going to have more time alone than she wanted. She hadn't passed a house in quite a while, if she remembered correctly.

The snow hadn't bothered her as long as she'd been safe and dry in her car. But she couldn't stay in her car. She had to find shelter before the storm got worse, as it seemed to be doing. Otherwise, she'd freeze to death.

With a powerful shove of her shoulder, she managed to budge the door and squeeze through the partial opening. Cold air assailed her, piercing the long sweater she wore over her T-shirt and jeans. The canvas sneakers already felt wet. She looked longingly at the car's interior after she'd reached back inside for her purse. No, she couldn't crawl back inside. She had to find help.

Wrapping her arms around herself in an attempt to hold in what little body heat she had, Jessica began climbing the incline her car had just slid down. The footing was treacherous and she fell several times, requiring her to free her hands to catch herself. The ache in her fingers warned her of the increasing cold.

When she finally reached the road again, she set out in the direction she'd come, pushing against the wind, her head bowed.

Some time later—she wasn't sure how long—she looked back over her shoulder, as if someone had tapped her there. She gasped as she discovered a small one-lane track heading into the woods.

Should she follow this little road? She certainly didn't remember seeing any houses on the highway; maybe she'd have better luck on the wooded route.

Once she started down the track, it seemed the strength of the storm eased. The tree limbs sheltered the track and the snow wasn't as deep. Her gratitude for the shelter was offset by the darkness those same limbs ensured. Soon, she lost any hint of civilization, the road being out of sight or sound.

The farther she walked, the more eerie the forest became. What if there was no house at the end of this little road? What if she was only putting greater distance between herself and any help? What if...?

"What if you stop imagining such silliness," she warned herself, even with her teeth clenched to keep from chattering.

She almost laughed at her situation. After all, she'd left her father's house, a huge mansion in an elite neighborhood of Kansas City, so she could be alone. Now she'd gotten her wish. She couldn't be more alone than she was right now.

Be careful what you wish for.

When she stumbled around a turn in the small road, she almost fell to her knees. There it was. A house. Gathering her strength, she hurried to the front door, under a wide overhang that gave protection from the snow.

Banging on the door, she waited impatiently for an answer. But the only sound she heard was that of her own labored breathing. After knocking again, she moved to the window and tried to peek in, but she couldn't see anything for the frosty snow on the panes. She returned to the door and turned the handle. Locked, of course.

What now? Should she break in? *Could* she? As cold as she was, she couldn't bring herself to break a window and crawl through.

With desperation, she left the shelter of the porch and circled the house, past the two-car garage, both locked, and around to the back door. When she tried it, she almost fell on her face as the door swung open.

Jessica quietly closed the door behind her, reveling in the warmth that filled the room. The kitchen was shadowy and dark, with no assistance from the outside. Flipping a light switch, she blinked rapidly at the sudden brightness that flooded the room.

"Hello?" she called in a wavering voice. Her fear filled her with disgust. She wasn't doing anything wrong. Well, not really. She hadn't broken in. The door was unlocked. And she was sure the owners wouldn't mind when they realized she would soon be suffering from hypothermia and starvation without their help.

"Hello?" she called again in a much stronger voice.

The response was the same. Nothing.

Her stomach growled and she decided to placate that part of her physical discomfort first. In the refrigerator, she discovered a bowl of macaroni and cheese neatly covered in plastic wrap. And not much else. A quick glance around the room located a microwave and she carried the bowl to it and started the warming process.

"It's only leftovers," she assured herself. Most people never ate them anyway. And she'd leave money to repay them.

Greedily she took the bowl from the microwave, found a fork and sat down at the table. Her outlook improved immediately when warm food reached her stomach.

After her quick meal, she put the bowl and fork into the sink and set out to address her other needs—warmth and dryness. By then maybe her hosts would be home and she could repay them and get them to take her to the nearest town.

What a relief!

ROB BERENSON, both hands full, pushed his way through the door leading from the garage to the kitchen. "Don't trip on the steps," he called back to his helpers.

"We won't, Daddy," Cathy assured him, her six-year-old voice full of confidence. She entered the kitchen right behind him, a grocery sack snug against her narrow chest.

Michael, the four-year-old, followed his sister with a huge package of toilet paper in his arms. The squeezable kind.

"Great, guys. Now, you start putting things away and I'll bring in the rest of the groceries."

"I want to help you, Daddy," Michael protested. "I'm a big boy."

"You sure are, Michael. But you're still the smallest of us three. Besides, boys have to put away groceries just like girls. Unless you want to give up eating." He didn't want his children to have sexist stereotypes.

At least he hoped they wouldn't. Parenting was a new role for him, and he wanted to do it right.

Michael, instead of being impressed with his father's words, slumped against the cabinet. "Cathy's bossy! I want to help you."

Rob quirked one eyebrow his way. "Do as I said, Michael." He let out a small sigh of relief when the little boy followed his orders.

After three more trips out to the garage, Rob had emptied his four-wheel-drive vehicle of their purchases, and the children were doing a good job of storing away their supplies.

"Daddy, you left a dirty bowl in the sink," Cathy said as he entered with the last bags.

"No, I didn't," he muttered, trying to remember if he'd forgotten anything they would need for the next few days. He hadn't counted on a snowstorm.

"Yes, you did. And it's right there." Cathy nodded toward the sink as she continued to stack cans in the pantry. "Mommy always tells us to put our dishes in the dishwasher."

Since she was so insistent, he peered into the sink and discovered his daughter was right. As usual. In just a few days, he'd realized her incredible memory and persistent pursuit of what she thought was right might drive him crazy.

"Michael, why didn't you put your bowl in the dishwasher?" he asked.

"I didn't eat nothin', Daddy," Michael assured him. "And I'm starved."

As usual. The child seemed to be a bottomless pit. "There's some leftover macaroni and cheese from lunch in the refrigerator. Why don't you heat it up in the microwave? That'll keep you going until dinner." Better macaroni than cookies, which he'd discovered was Michael's favorite treat.

"What do I get, Daddy?" Cathy asked, her hands on her hips in indignation.

"Michael will share with you, honey."

"I can't," Michael replied, his head stuck in the refrigerator.

"Now, Michael, we've talked about sharing. If your sister wants some, you—"

"I can't 'cause it's gone."

Rob looked over his shoulder, irritated. "Don't be silly, son. I put it in there after lunch."

Cathy ran to the refrigerator. "Michael's right, Daddy. It's gone. You must've eaten it."

"Of course I didn't. We went to town right after lunch. Don't you—" He paused and then turned back to the sink. The empty bowl, full of water now, had held the macaroni when they'd left the house.

Rob plopped down into one of the chairs at the table to think and then leaped to his feet. "What the—"

"Daddy, how come your pants are all wet?" Cathy asked.

Michael covered his mouth with his hands. "Daddy, did you have an accident?"

Since Michael occasionally had accidents of the bathroom variety, his accusation wasn't a surprise, but Rob stared in astonishment at what he could see of the rear of his khaki slacks. They were soaked.

He ran his hand over the chair cushion, discovering its condition matched that of his pants. Then he stared at the ceiling, expecting to discover a leak. After all, it had been raining off and on for several weeks before the snow came.

But the kitchen ceiling was unblemished.

Cathy came toward the table and skidded, almost losing her balance. "Daddy, the floor's wet, too."

Rob glowered at the evidence before him. Obviously someone had come into their cabin. He crossed to the door that led to the back porch. As usual, it was unlocked. Since they'd gone out through the garage, he'd forgotten to lock that door.

"Um, kids, why don't you go get in the car. And lock the doors."

"Where are we going?" Michael asked.

"Nowhere. I just want to, uh, play a game."

"Is someone here?" Cathy asked, her voice a whisper.

"I don't think so, baby, but I want you two to be safe while I look around." No point in beating around the bush. Cathy would figure everything out anyway.

Her little chest swelled as she threw back her shoulders. "We'll come with you, Daddy, so we can protect you."

Rob couldn't fight back a grin. He was a real macho man when his six-year-old daughter thought she needed to take care of *him*. Especially when he thought about the job he'd just walked away from. "Thanks, honey, but I think—"

"I gotta go!" Michael announced and raced from the kitchen before Rob could move. Neither he nor Cathy needed further explanation.

"Michael, wait!" he called, racing after his son, Cathy hot on his heels.

Either Rob was out of shape, or Michael was faster than he'd thought a four-year-old could be. By the time he reached the staircase, Michael was at the top. Even as he climbed the stairs, Rob noticed the wet footprints on the carpet.

Someone—a stranger—was upstairs, where his son was going. "Cathy, go back to the truck. I'll get Michael."

Though she usually obeyed him, his daughter didn't bother this time. Instead she clutched his hand and climbed with him. Together, they followed Michael to the bathroom.

Cathy waited outside the door to spare Michael's modesty. Too bad Michael didn't have any.

"I made it, Daddy!" his son announced, beaming up at him.

Rob cleared his throat. "Uh, good, Michael."

Cathy whispered around the door. "Is there anyone in there, Daddy?"

Her words reminded Rob of the reason for his furious chase. "No, baby, just Michael. Michael, when you finish, go back downstairs with Cathy."

He'd noticed the wet footsteps had gone to the bedroom on the right, the one he was using. He returned to the hallway. "You wait here for Michael and then both of you go back downstairs."

Cathy's unhappy face told him she didn't like his orders, but she didn't protest.

Rob followed the wet footprints to the room on the right. He reached down and opened the door just as he heard rustling behind him. He spun around to find his children rushing to join him.

"Is anyone there?" Cathy asked in a loud whisper.

Though he'd opened the door, Rob's attention had

been directed to his children. Now he swung around to the room before him even as he began, "No, I don't think—"

"Daddy, there's a naked lady in the bed!" Michael interrupted him.

Rob's gaze focused on the item of furniture mentioned in Michael's unbelievable words and he discovered his son was right. There was a naked lady in his bed. A beautiful naked lady.

Their voices had awakened her and she stared at them, her wide blue eyes huge, one visible bare shoulder creamy smooth. Then, as reaction set in, she rolled to her knees and clutched the comforter to her.

Michael had been right. Beneath that comforter was only flesh and bone, a most enticing package from what Rob could tell. She was definitely naked.

"Who are you?" she demanded in a shaky voice.

His children looked at him.

He cleared his throat. "Don't you think that should be our line? After all, this is our place."

"Oh." Her skin flooded with color, contrasting with her pale gold hair. She sank back down against the pillows. His pillows. An immediate vision of sharing his space with this stranger had him clearing his throat again.

Cathy tugged on his shirt.

He looked down, reluctantly withdrawing his stare from the stranger. "Hmm?"

"Daddy," she whispered. "It's Goldilocks."

Michael's eyes got even larger. "Did the bears chase you here?" he asked their unexpected visitor.

"No, silly," Cathy replied before the woman could. "We're the bears! Right, Daddy?"

Rob shook his head but he couldn't hide his grin. He'd told the children they were going to be the three bears in the woods this weekend. With the last name of Berenson, his teasing had caught the children's imagination more than he'd thought.

"That's a fairy tale, Cathy. You'd better take Michael down to the kitchen and finish putting away the groceries while I find out why we have a visitor."

"But, Daddy, she ate our macaroni, sat in our chairs and slept in your bed, just like Goldilocks."

"Goldilocks slept in Baby Bear's bed, not Papa Bear's," Rob protested and then felt his cheeks redden as he thought of the woman in his bed.

"Maybe she got confused," Cathy replied, ignoring her father's embarrassment. She smiled at their unexpected guest. "Don't be afraid. We're not really bears."

The woman offered a tentative smile at Cathy, but her wariness returned when she looked at Rob again.

"Cathy, take Michael downstairs for a cupcake and some milk." He knew he shouldn't use food as bribery, but it was so doggone effective.

Michael, hungry as always, took his sister's hand and began tugging in the direction of the staircase. Rob had learned he could always count on his son to respond to food.

"But, Daddy—"

"Cathy, do as I say." Rob tried to make his voice

stern though he doubted if he fooled Cathy. But the two children went down the stairs.

The woman must've believed his threatening stance. Her eyes grew rounder with alarm and she clutched the comforter more tightly to her.

Which was a good thing, because if she dropped it, he might stand there and drool.

Once he was sure his children were out of earshot, Rob prompted her. "Well?"

She didn't misunderstand his demand for an explanation. "It's snowing."

When she said nothing else, he replied, "I can assure you it's not the first time it's snowed here. But never before have we found a naked lady in one of our beds."

He knew he had the advantage, especially since he was wearing clothes, but he crossed his arms over his chest and waited, trying out his stern expression on her.

"I— My car went in a ditch."

Her eyes were as blue as the sky and as big as saucers.

"Where?"

"I don't know," she suddenly wailed, losing her composure. "It felt like miles away, but walking in the cold may have made it seem longer. The snow made the road slippery. The car started spinning, and before I knew what was happening, I went over the side. The car was stuck. I couldn't stay there because there was no traffic and I was afraid I'd freeze to death. So I started walking. I th-thought I was going to die. Then I found your house."

Several tears had slid down her beautiful cheeks, and she clutched the comforter as if it were a lifeline.

"You're lucky you didn't freeze," he said gruffly, hoping to hide the fact that her distress had touched him.

She nodded but said nothing. Apparently she'd used up all her conversation in her explanation.

His gaze drifted over her bare shoulders. Snapping his thoughts from such distractions, he asked, "Where are your clothes?"

"I—I hung them on the steam heater," she said, gesturing toward the enclosed heater against the wall. "The snow melted all the way through to my skin."

To avoid thinking about the aforementioned soft, smooth skin, he stared at the heater. A small pair of jeans hung on the back of a chair in front of it. A lacy pair of bikini panties with a matching bra, along with a pair of socks, were resting on the pipes. He forced his gaze away from such intimate apparel and discovered a T-shirt spread on the seat of the chair. Under it rested a pair of tennis shoes. Hanging from the curtain rod on a hanger was a long cardigan sweater.

"I—I borrowed a hanger from your closet."

It was all still soaked.

All Rob knew was he needed to get some clothes on the lady at once. For his peace of mind if nothing else.

He walked toward the old dresser, sparing his visitor a glance. She didn't appear to have moved.

Throwing open a dresser drawer, he pulled out a pair of old sweatpants and a sweatshirt. Neither would fit the woman, but the pants had a drawstring. He added a pair of athletic socks. At the back of the drawer he found a package of silk bikini briefs his ex-wife had bought for him that he'd refused to wear.

"Put these on," he said, tossing all of his finds to the bed. "Then gather up your things and come downstairs. I'll take you to Jackson." At her puzzled look, he added, "The nearest town."

He escaped from the room before she could agree or protest his high-handedness. He assured himself he wasn't interested in her response. After all, he hadn't dealt with a woman's quixotic behavior in quite a while—and he hadn't missed it.

As he reached the bottom of the stairs, he was met by Cathy and Michael.

"Is the pretty lady going to stay?" Cathy asked.

"No, she's not," he said firmly. "As soon as she's dressed, we're going to take her to town. Put on your shoes and coats again. And, Michael, take a trip to the bathroom before we leave. You need to wash away your chocolate mustache."

"I don't have a mustache, do I, Daddy?" Cathy asked as Michael ran up the stairs.

"No, sweetheart, you're just about perfect," he assured her, kissing her forehead. Those same words might also describe the lady upstairs. But his reaction to her hadn't been fatherly.

He cleared his throat. "Go get ready."

Because the sooner he rid his home of the temptation he'd found in his bed, the happier he'd be. He had a different agenda for this weekend, one that was more important than time spent with a beautiful woman.

A fleeting vision of the temptress in his bed made him question his decision, but he shook his head. Nope. Any social life would come later, much later, he realized, as his children came running back down the stairs. No beautiful blonde with big blue eyes was going to disrupt his plans.

What was he worrying about? he suddenly asked himself with a grin. No self-respecting beauty would even want to hang around with him and two kids. Besides, Cathy called her Goldilocks. If he remembered his fairy tales correctly, the first thing Goldilocks had done was run away.

Maybe he'd growl a little just to be on the safe side.

Chapter Two

Jessica Barnes stared at the empty door, where she'd last seen the man. Finally her gaze dropped to the clothing he'd tossed on the bed.

With a shrug of her shoulders, she held the comforter with one hand and drew the sweatshirt toward her with the other. Not exactly haute couture, but she was desperate.

After another cautious look at the empty doorway, she dropped the comforter to her waist and hurriedly pulled the sweatshirt over her head. Almost immediately her spirits rose. What a difference clothing made.

Of course, in other circumstances, being without clothing might not be so demoralizing. She immediately dismissed the picture of her reluctant host that popped into her head. He was a handsome man.

But she wasn't interested. She had other problems to deal with. And his haste to rid himself of her said he also wanted her gone.

Not that she blamed him. What if his wife had found her in his bed, naked? She hadn't really given much thought to such things when she'd taken shelter from the snowstorm. She hadn't even intended to go to sleep. She'd just been trying to keep warm.

She opened the still-sealed package of underwear and pulled out a pair of bright blue silk briefs. Slipping them on under the covers, she soon added the sweatpants. Only then did she completely abandon the comforter.

After pulling on the thick socks, she got out of bed and carefully remade it. Even in her frozen state, she'd taken in how neat and clean everything was. It would be ungrateful not to return the bed to its pristine state.

Then she checked her own underwear. Her bra would've been...convenient, but it was still wet. Which meant she hadn't been asleep all that long.

With a sigh, she folded her wet garments into a tidy stack, then picking up her shoes and purse, she hurried down the stairs. The two children were standing at the bottom, watching her every move, as if they'd never seen a woman before.

"Where's your father?" she asked them.

"He's on the telephone. There was a call," the girl said, her gaze never leaving Jessica.

Some kind of movement must have drawn her gaze because she saw her reluctant host through a doorway in what looked to be a den, holding a telephone receiver.

"What?" he said with a ferocious frown. "But, Jack—*damn it!*" After a brief pause, he added, "Yeah, thanks for calling." He hung up the phone.

The little girl covered her mouth, her eyes widening even more. The boy grabbed his sister's arm. "What's that mean?"

"Daddy said a bad word," she told her brother in a whisper that the adults could easily hear.

"And how do you know that's a bad word?" her father demanded as he came to the door, staring at his daughter.

She dropped her gaze. "Mrs. Hutchins said it was when Mr. Hutchins said it."

"Mr. Hutchins talks like that around you?" The man was still frowning.

"Only once. When he hit his thumb with the hammer."

Jessica immediately pictured the poor man with his thumb throbbing and his wife wanting to wash his mouth out with soap. She couldn't hold back a grin.

Until she met the man's glare.

"Um, who are the Hutchinses?" she asked to distract him.

"An older couple who look after the kids," he explained, but he still seemed unhappy with everyone.

"Oh. Well, I'm ready," she announced, hoping to change the subject.

"We're not going anywhere," he growled and began pacing the hallway.

Suspicions that had arisen in her when he'd sent his children away a few minutes earlier filled her head. "Why not?" she demanded.

"Is she going to stay?" Cathy asked, excitement in her voice.

The man frowned at her, distracted by something. "I checked outside. It's snowing worse than before and shows no sign of letting up. My neighbor just called with word that they've shut down parts of the highway, too. We'll have to wait until it stops."

Without another word, he turned and walked away from them.

"Wait!" Jessica called after she'd recovered from the shock. He ignored her and disappeared behind a swinging door.

"Isn't that the kitchen?" she asked the children.

"Yes. You want to see?" Cathy offered.

"I most assuredly do. I want to see your father and get an explanation." She wasn't used to being ignored. "He has very bad manners."

She regretted her own lapse in manners when the little boy frowned at her.

"He's a good daddy," he protested.

"Of course he is, sweetie. I just don't understand how long he meant when he said we'd have to wait."

"I think he meant until the snow stops," Cathy explained.

Hysterical laughter bubbled up inside her and Jessica worked to maintain control. She didn't want to hurt the little girl's feelings. "Yes, I think you're right, but I need to ask your daddy a few more questions. So can we go to the kitchen?"

When the trio opened the door to the kitchen, the man was staring out the window over the sink. He must've heard the door opening because he spun around and stared at them.

Jessica didn't like the feeling of imposing on strangers. She hadn't asked to have her Mercedes slide into a ditch, to wander in the storm for a long time, to wind up in a stranger's house, with not a stitch of dry clothing to call her own. She started to tell the man he would be well rewarded for whatever help he offered, but something in the set of his shoulders made her hold back the words.

"Excuse me," she began stiltedly, "could you be a little more forthcoming about the situation? What did you mean, until the storm is over?"

To her surprise, he laughed. "You don't understand English?"

She wanted to stomp her foot. But she didn't. "Of course I do. But how long will that be?"

"I don't know. I haven't heard a recent weather report."

She stared at him, his cavalier air different from the earlier eagerness to see the end of her. "Can you guess how long we'll be trapped here?"

He stiffened slightly. "I don't think I'd call this place a trap. But we can't connect with the rest of society, if that's what you mean. Except by phone." He paused and then added, as if he feared she might be worried, "But it's okay. We have plenty of food."

Jessica clutched her purse to her as she considered the aspects of their situation. The children were staring at her as she mulled over his words. Trapped. A pleasant trap. Much nicer than the one she'd run away from.

She smiled at her host. "I apologize for imposing

on you. Of course,'' she added, sure now that he wouldn't be offended, ''I'll pay you for the temporary lodging for however long we'll be here.''

His eyes narrowed. ''You don't seem upset.''

Upset? No, actually she was relieved. But she wasn't going to share that thought with her host. ''Well, there's no point in crying about something that can't be changed.''

''I thought you'd be anxious to get away.''

Jessica decided she'd better backtrack. The man seemed unhappy with her reaction. ''Well, of course, it's inconvenient, but—''

''Don't you have a job? Or someone waiting for you?'' He paused, staring at her. ''Maybe they could bring in a helicopter. As soon as the snow stops.''

Her eyes widened. She hadn't thought of that. She'd have to keep her exact location secret. ''Surely we're not in such desperate straits. Do you mind having company for a day or two? Will your wife—''

''We don't have a wife,'' Cathy immediately said.

Laughing, Jessica replied, ''Good, because I think you're much too young for marriage.'' She and the little girl chuckled together, but she realized the man hadn't participated in their humor when she looked back at him. Something about his rigidity irritated her.

''Perhaps, since we're going to be together for a while, we should introduce ourselves,'' she suggested, watching him. ''My name is Jessica Barnes.''

As though reluctant to reveal anything about himself or his children, the man finally said, "I'm Rob Berenson and these are my children, Cathy and Michael."

"I'm Cathy," the little girl added.

"Thank you for telling me," Jessica teased. "I might have called you Michael." She and Cathy exchanged grins.

"Our name is why Daddy says we're the bears," Cathy added, when Jessica gave her a blank look. "Don't you get it? *Bear*-enson?"

"Oh, of course. Well, you certainly don't look like bears," she said to Cathy, teasing her. Her glance then flew to her host and she wondered if she should take those words back. He was frowning at her, about as friendly as a grizzly bear.

"We'll probably be able to get you to town tomorrow if the snow stops," Rob Berenson hurriedly assured her, taking Cathy's hand and pulling her closer to him. As if Jessica had a communicable disease.

His behavior irritated her. "Will it help if I assure you I'm not a wanted criminal or a monster? I won't hurt your children."

"I'm not worried about my children," he assured her huskily.

The tone of his voice evoked visions of his bed and what could occur in it. Without thinking first, she offered the reassurance her wayward thoughts needed. "Then you must be worried about yourself. If I promise not to ravish you, Mr. Berenson, will it relieve your mind?"

"Perhaps you're the one who should be asking for promises, Miss Barnes."

ROB GLARED AT THE WOMAN. How dare she tease him? How dare she seem relieved that she would be staying? How dare she stand there and look so beautiful?

His words had been mean, but he was the bear in this little scenario, wasn't he?

When her rosy cheeks paled, he felt more like a bully. But she'd asked for it.

"Daddy, what's 'ravish'?" Cathy asked, seemingly unaware of the tension between the two adults.

He stared at his sweet daughter, unable to come up with an explanation. "Since our guest is the one who used that word, maybe she'd like to explain."

He should've known better.

She took Cathy's hand and bent down to say in a low voice, "It's kissing and mushy stuff like that. Some men are afraid of women, you know."

"Daddy's not afraid of nothin'," Michael said, moving to stand by his father.

Michael was wrong, Rob admitted. He would be petrified to kiss their guest—because he knew he might lose control. He was already too attracted to her.

"Maybe we should try the roads after all. They might not be too bad," he suggested, desperate to separate this woman from his family.

All of his audience stared at him.

"But, Daddy, it hasn't stopped snowing," Cathy finally spoke for everyone. "Why would the roads be any better? We slid lots when we were coming home.''

Man, he was in bad shape when he couldn't even fool a six-year-old. ''Never mind. If you want to use the phone, it's—''

''I know. I saw you talking earlier. But there's no rush. I'll call later.''

Rob frowned again. Why didn't she want to make a phone call? It seemed odd to him that she wasn't interested in contacting *someone*. He shook his head. He'd left his job. It wasn't any of his business.

''I hate to be a difficult guest,'' she continued, ''but—are we going to eat anytime soon? I'm starving.''

''But you ate our macaroni and cheese,'' Michael said pointedly.

For the first time since she'd gotten dressed, the young woman seemed embarrassed. ''I know. I hope you didn't mind, but I had skipped lunch and—and—''

Cathy squeezed her hand. ''It's okay. Michael didn't mind 'cause Daddy let us have a cupcake instead.''

''Oh, good.''

She actually seemed relieved at Cathy's reassurance, Rob realized.

She turned and caught him watching her. With another beautiful smile, she asked, ''Will seventy-five a day be enough?''

He stared at her, confused. ''What?''

''Will seventy-five dollars a day be enough?''

"Enough for what?" He seemed to have lost track of the conversation.

"Enough compensation for my stay." She smiled, as if what she'd just said was normal.

"No, it won't."

She arched her eyebrows. "Very well. A hundred?"

His eyes narrowed again. She didn't seem the least bit concerned about throwing money around. "Do you have money to burn?"

She stiffened. "I'm trying to negotiate my fee."

"Well, you don't negotiate by raising the amount, unless the other guy is paying. Someone neglected to instruct you in how to go about it. And they also didn't teach you about polite behavior. We don't ask our guests to pay."

Her cheeks flushed, she glared at him. "I'm not a tightwad. You don't really have a choice about my company, so I'm trying to be fair."

"Here's fair. Put your money someplace where it's wanted. You'll be our guest until we can get you out of here." He added under his breath, "Which I hope will be soon."

"I beg your pardon?" She glared at him, her spine rigid. "I didn't hear that last part."

He should've known. Maybe persistence was a female trait instead of just Cathy's. It hadn't been one his wife had shared, but clearly their guest wasn't going to let go. "I said I hoped we'd have you out of here soon."

"I'm sorry my stay is so unpleasant to you. Is there a corner you want me to sit in? Or perhaps you'd like me to stay in a closet until the world thaws out.''

"Don't be ridiculous. Tomorrow is Thanksgiving. I thought you'd want to be with your family." He turned away and opened the refrigerator. Time to change the subject before she began wondering why he didn't want her around. "We're having fried chicken for dinner."

A low growl was her response, and he turned to stare at her.

Her cheeks were flaming. "My—my stomach growled. I'm sorry, but I'm very hungry. Uh, who's going to cook it?"

He couldn't keep from smiling at her. At least she wouldn't be one of those women who picked at their food. "It's already cooked. Dinner's coming right up."

JESSICA WATCHED her host remove a box from the refrigerator and put the pieces of fried chicken inside it on a plate. Her stomach welcomed the quickness of his meal preparations.

"We bought fried chicken on the way home since we took so long to shop," he explained as he caught her hungry stare.

"I'm glad. I don't think I could last any longer."

"Sounds like Michael. He's always hungry, right, son?"

Michael nodded and hid behind his father's leg, as if embarrassed.

Jessica frowned. "Um, who comes in to do the cooking, normally? And the cleaning?"

The man stared at her, one eyebrow slipping up. "You're looking at him. This isn't a palace you've found in the woods."

"I just assumed— Never mind. Of course not."

Cathy stood beside the chair Jessica had taken. The little girl reached out and stroked Jessica's hair, and she turned to look at Cathy.

"Sorry. But your hair is so pretty."

"That's all right. But yours is just as pretty. I like your braids."

"Daddy helped me, but he doesn't know how very well." They both looked at the man, but he was putting potato salad in a bowl.

"I can teach you to French braid it if you want," Jessica said.

"Daddy! Jessica's going to show me how to French braid my hair!" Cathy announced, bouncing up and down in excitement.

He frowned but only said, "That's nice. You and Michael need to set the table. The first drawer on the other side of the sink."

"I'll help," Jessica offered at once. She felt guilty at not offering to assist in the meal preparations, but she'd been raised with servants to meet her every need. It was hard to remember to do things herself.

Cathy beamed at her offer, but Rob said nothing. Jessica could feel his eyes on her as she followed Cathy to the drawer where the silverware was located.

"That's too many forks," Cathy protested as Jessica picked them up. "There's just four of us. You have eight forks."

Embarrassed, Jessica immediately replaced the salad forks she had chosen as a matter of course. Even breakfast at her house required a full complement of silver.

"Cathy counts very well," Rob said softly and she raised her gaze to his.

He knew. She guessed it was an easy thing to figure out, but it embarrassed her just the same. "Um, napkins?"

"That's Michael's job," Cathy assured her.

"In the pantry, son," Rob added.

When they reached the table with the silverware, Michael was going around the table with a box of paper napkins, carefully removing one and putting it on the table by each chair. Jessica was glad she hadn't said anything about cloth napkins, like she always used at home.

Jessica carefully watched Cathy for her cue, as if she were in a foreign land. The little girl turned to her father. "Where are the glasses?"

"Here, I'll get them," he said and set four glasses on the cabinet.

Jessica stared at Cathy and then her father. "Wait a minute. Why don't the kids know where anything is? I thought you said this was your house." She had sudden visions of a kidnapping or something equally frightening.

"It is. My grandparents' house originally. I use it as a fishing cabin now. I brought the kids here for Thanksgiving. We were going to have a real family holiday."

The implication that she was ruining everything

hung in the air. "It wasn't my intention to disrupt your plans," she said stiffly.

He gave her a lopsided grin and shrugged his shoulders. Not a huge reassurance, but at least he hadn't kicked her out in the snow.

"Okay, guys, come fill your plates," Rob ordered as Cathy finished carrying the glasses to the table.

Jessica stood back and noticed the children did as he said with no fear on their faces. They seemed to trust him. Slightly relieved, she took a plate and filled it, then followed the children to the table. They patiently waited—even Michael—and in spite of her growling stomach, Jessica followed suit.

When Rob sat down, he and the children took each other's hands. She took Cathy's hand, a questioning look on her face. When Rob reached for her hand before bowing his head, she allowed him to take it and closed her eyes for the blessing.

It touched her, that warm little hand on one side curled up in hers, a sense of trust and friendship that she hadn't experienced in a long time. In fact, such innocence hadn't come her way recently.

On the other side, Rob's hand evoked a different reaction. She was stunned by the heat, the electricity that coursed through her. Though she tried to ignore such a strange reaction, the shiver that ran through her was real.

When she opened her eyes and raised her head, immediately snatching her hand from his, she discovered her host staring at her. She offered him a tentative smile, hoping he hadn't noticed her strange reaction, unsure what his response would be.

He smiled back and nodded to her plate. "Now you can eat."

She tried to act as if she weren't hungry. That's how she'd been raised. To always maintain good manners even if you're dying. With the first bite of fried chicken, however, she closed her eyes and savored the tender meat with the crunchy crust. Nothing had ever tasted so good.

"Do you like it?" Cathy asked.

Jessica opened her eyes and smiled. "Oh, yes. It tastes wonderful."

"It's probably not what you're used to. It's not exactly caviar," Rob commented, giving her a knowing stare.

She shrugged her shoulders. She wasn't that fond of caviar anyway.

"What's caviar?" Cathy asked, looking at her father.

"It's fish eggs."

"Fish eggs? *Eewh!* Why would anyone eat that?"

"Do fish have nests?" Michael asked.

Jessica munched on her chicken and left Rob to answer his children's questions. After all, he was the one who'd aroused their curiosity.

Cathy, however, wasn't about to leave her out of the conversation. "Do you like fish eggs, Jessica?"

"Not very much, but I've eaten them."

"Have you, Daddy?" the persistent Cathy demanded.

"Yes."

"Will we have to eat them?"

"Not unless you want to," Jessica assured her.

"Caviar is very expensive. Most people don't mind if you don't want to eat any."

"Is it as expensive as chicken?" Michael asked.

"More," Rob said, grinning at his son.

"Then I'll just have another drumstick, okay, Daddy?"

"Suits me, Michael. With your appetite I'd go broke buying caviar."

They finished the meal with little additional conversation. Jessica was satisfied to eat. She hadn't been that hungry in her entire life. In fact, all her senses seemed enhanced, whether because of her hunger or not.

When she finished, wiping her mouth with her napkin, she discovered the others watching her.

"Do you want some more chicken?" Cathy asked, playing the rôle of hostess.

"No, thank you, Cathy, but that was a wonderful meal."

The little girl giggled. "It's lots better than Daddy's fried chicken."

"Thanks a lot, kid," Rob muttered.

"Is your fried chicken good?" Cathy asked Jessica, ignoring her father.

"Um, I've never fried a chicken," Jessica confessed.

"Can you make cookies?" Michael asked.

Jessica shrugged her shoulders and shook her head, inadequacy filling her. It wasn't a comfortable feeling.

"Enough, kids. Jessica's not applying for a housekeeping job. She's a guest. And I don't think she's used to waiting on herself, much less anyone else.''

His words weren't a question, but his gaze was.

Well, too bad. She wasn't about to confess anything! Experience had taught her that telling him her problem or about her father would only create more difficulties for her.

Chapter Three

"Well? Am I right?" Rob watched her, a small smile pulling at the corners of his lips.

"About what, Daddy?" Cathy asked, a puzzled look on her face.

"I don't know what you're talking about," Jessica said, attempting to hide her reaction to his question. She wasn't going to tell anyone she came from a wealthy family. She'd learned the hard way how important her money was to others.

The man opposite her didn't press her for an answer. Instead he brought up another difficult subject. "While we do the dishes, why don't you go call your family and let them know you're all right."

"Nonsense. I know enough about manners—contrary to your earlier remarks—to offer to help with the dishes." She raised her chin in challenge.

"We don't need any help."

"Yes, we do, Daddy," Cathy quickly contradicted. "Jessica can help me and Michael clear the table."

"You should call her Miss Barnes, Cathy."

"No!" Jessica quickly countered. "I'd like Cathy

and Michael to call me Jessica." It seemed to her the man was always trying to put some distance between her and his children.

"What about me? Don't I get to call you Jessica, too?" he asked, taking her by surprise. Not only was he teasing her, but his words were accompanied by a smile.

"Of—of course."

"And you'll call me Rob?"

"That would be easier than Mr. Berenson," she agreed. And before she could stop it, an involuntary smile lit her face.

"What's the matter, don't you like my name?" Rob teased.

As they all cleaned, the four of them recalled the worst names they'd heard. Rob teased his children with the possibilities and all of them roared with laughter.

Jessica enjoyed the lightheartedness. Even more, she was relieved that the topic of calling her family was dropped. She had no intention of letting anyone know where she was.

"I know! I know!" Cathy shouted, dancing up and down. "Hippopotamus! Michael Hippopotamus!"

"Or Ant. Cathy Ant," Rob suggested. "Isn't there some rock star with the name Ant?"

"Yes, but I think he made it up," Jessica told him.

"Why would he do that?" Cathy asked.

"Some people make up names so no one will find

them.'' Rob directed the reply to Cathy but he stared at Jessica, as if accusing her of that very thing.

She stared back, irritated by his behavior. She hadn't lied about anything! Maybe Mr. Berenson was the one who was hiding. She thought again about his children not knowing where anything was in the house. His explanation had been smooth, but what if it was a lie? What if he'd stolen his kids and lied to them? Her eyes widened as she returned his stare.

Suddenly he looked away and said, ''It's bath-time, kids. Go upstairs and get out your clean pa-jamas and underwear and I'll come run your bath-water. You first, Michael, and then Cathy.''

The sudden change in Rob was unsettling. One moment he was laughing and teasing, the next he'd become stern and unwelcoming. What did she know about this man? Had he revealed any more about himself than she had of her life? Was she crazy to trust a stranger?

The two children left the kitchen, but Jessica fig-ured they'd been sent away because Rob was wor-ried about what she might ask. She didn't intend to disappoint him. ''Where is the children's mother?''

''Hmm?'' Rob wiped down the kitchen counter, not bothering to look at her.

She repeated her question, but she wondered if asking was smart. What if he'd ''disposed'' of her? Would she, Jessica, be next?

''She's in South America.''

A chill ran up her spine. ''South America?'' she

repeated. Unconsciously she stepped back until she realized what she was doing.

"Yeah. Her husband was transferred."

"How convenient." She clapped a hand over her mouth as if she could cancel her sarcastic remark.

He put the dishcloth across the sink divider and turned to face her, his hands on his hips. "What's that supposed to mean?"

His challenging stance, the muscles he flexed, his hazel eyes, all distracted her. But she wasn't going to back down. "It makes it a little hard to verify, that's all."

A puzzled look spread across his face before a slow grin took its place. "Aha! You suspect me of some dastardly deed, don't you? What did I do? Bury her in the backyard before I snatched my kids?"

She stiffened. He was laughing at her. "It's been known to happen. Were you in a custody suit?"

"Nope," he replied, his grin still in place. "We happily divorced, she happily remarried and happily moved to South America, leaving our children in my care."

"No one is that happily divorced."

"You've been watching too much television. I have to go supervise bathtime. You go call your family and assure them you're stuck here with an ax-murderer." With those words of advice, which sounded more like an order to her, he left the kitchen.

She followed him to the bottom of the stairs, watching his taut buns as he loped up the stairs. The man was in good condition, no doubt about it, ax-murderer or no ax-murderer.

And dictatorial, as well. Like her father.

Only this time, her father had gone too far.

She returned to the kitchen and took a letter from her purse. Her mother's letter to her father, written over twenty years earlier. It had been packed away in the attic after her mother's death seven years ago.

Slowly she unfolded the yellowed paper, her gaze scanning the words of love and commitment. When she'd read it for the first time just last week, she'd realized at once what had been troubling her.

She wasn't in love.

Not the kind of love her mother had felt for her father. Not the kind of love a woman should feel for a man when she commits her life to him. Not a forever kind of love.

But she was engaged.

When the truth had finally become clear to her, she'd raced to her father, sure he would support her as he'd done throughout her life. She'd taken him the letter she'd found.

But John Barnes had been irritated by her "sentimentality," dismissing her sudden fears as last-minute jitters. He'd pointed out how well Stephen fit in their family, how caring he was of Jessica, how eager he was to marry.

Jessica wandered back to the foot of the stairs and sat down, waiting for Rob to reappear, as she considered her father's response. She had considered the things her father had said. But she feared, as much as she hated to admit it, that he was motivated by something other than her welfare. He'd been difficult of late, worried. Then, when Stephen had appeared on the scene, his black mood had lifted.

Stephen was all the things her father had said. But there was something about him—something she couldn't put her finger on—that bothered her. Maybe it was that he was all those things. Too perfect. As if he wasn't being himself.

It didn't matter. Once she realized she didn't love him, she knew she couldn't marry Stephen. No matter what her father said. But when she'd told him she was canceling the engagement and the engagement party scheduled the next week, he'd laughed and insisted she do no such thing.

She'd done it anyway.

He'd called and reinstated the orders.

She'd called Stephen and told him she wouldn't marry him. Her father had already contacted him. Stephen assured her of his love, but Jessica hadn't believed him. Now that she understood why she'd been worried, why she'd felt uneasy, why she'd been longing for someone to talk over her engagement with, she wasn't so easily fooled.

"But I don't love you, Stephen," she had replied quietly, firmly.

"Nonsense, Jessica. We get along fine."

"Marriage is not about getting along."

"Yes, it is. We both want the same things," Stephen had assured her. "A good future, family, security."

With a deep sigh, she had said, "I'm breaking our engagement, Stephen. I won't marry you."

A hard edge she hadn't heard before set into his voice. "Jessica, you're being foolish. Your father has assured me the party will go on as scheduled. Our engagement is going to be announced."

Her father thought he could run roughshod over her feelings because he wanted Stephen for a son-in-law. Was Stephen the son he'd never had, or was there another reason?

Without saying another word, Jessica had hung up the phone. The few times she'd disagreed with her father in the past, she'd discovered his determination. In the end, he'd always managed to win.

But this time the stakes were too high. She wasn't going to be forced into a marriage she didn't want. Quietly she'd gone along with the party plans so as not to arouse suspicion. Her father's staff was suddenly very attentive to her every move.

When she'd made up her mind to go away, she hadn't been able to take much with her—no suitcases. So she'd gotten in her car, stopped at the bank and withdrawn a lot of cash and driven off. And she was going to stay away until after the party.

She heard steps behind her, from her seat on the bottom stair, and spun around. "You're finished already?" she asked Rob.

"It's been half an hour. If they'd bathed much longer, they would've shriveled up. Did you make your phone call?"

"Yes, yes, I did," she assured him, keeping her gaze on the letter she was refolding.

"I forgot to give you the phone number here. Do

you want to call them back so they'll know how to reach you?''

"That's not necessary. They aren't worried about me.''

He didn't respond; he simply stood above her on the stairs. She got to her feet and turned to look at him.

"Well, they should be," he finally muttered.

"What do you mean?"

He let out a sigh of exasperation. "Jessica, you're a beautiful young woman from a wealthy family and, if I'm any judge of things, pretty naive. Don't you think that would cause any parent to be concerned?"

"I never said my family was wealthy!" she protested.

"Right," he drawled. "All women expect a staff of servants in a fishing cabin."

Her cheeks turned red at her earlier gaffe. She'd hoped he'd forgotten it. To distract him, she said, "I'm safe, here with you and Cathy and Michael." But the children were upstairs, and the look in Rob's eyes made her wonder if her words were true.

He stared at her, shaking his head. "I guess you don't believe I'm an ax-murderer, after all." With a grin, he added, "Cathy and Michael are going to watch a video in my room. Do you want to see *Cinderella* with them?"

"Yes, that would be fun. That's one of my favorite movies."

He grinned. "I should've known Goldilocks

would love Cinderella. It's kind of a sisterhood thing, isn't it?''

His teasing reassured her. She stuck out her tongue at him and started up the stairs, only to almost trip over her own feet at his next words.

''Do you want me to call your family and reassure them, give them my phone number?''

Without turning around, she swallowed and then said, ''No, that's not necessary. I promise you they aren't worried.''

''Jessica?''

The question in that one word enticed her to turn around. ''Yes, Rob?''

''You're sure?''

''Absolutely.'' She smiled but refrained from adding anything else. She'd once read that most liars gave themselves away by overexplaining. ''If you'll excuse me, I'm going to hurry up. I don't want to miss the movie.''

''All right, Goldilocks, run away.''

Though his words invited her to smile, she turned and hurried away from him instead.

When Jessica opened the door to Rob's room, where she'd taken her nap earlier in the day, she discovered Cathy and Michael in their pajamas, leaning against the pillows in the middle of the king-size bed. ''Your dad said I could watch the movie with you.''

Cathy immediately scooted over so Jessica could sit between them, her smile wide and inviting. Jessica stretched her arms around them as they snuggled up against her.

As the music and magic of the Disney movie wrapped itself around the three of them, Jessica thought she hadn't spent as pleasant an evening in a long time. But she did wonder what Rob was doing.

ROB SAT DOWN at the kitchen table and tried to make out a menu for Thanksgiving dinner the next day. It wasn't something he had a lot of experience with. Had he made a mistake bringing the kids here for the holiday?

He would've said no until Goldilocks appeared.

Shoving a hand through his hair, he chuckled at his imagination. After all, what could one beautiful woman do to mess things up? Maybe he should ask Helen of Troy's husband that question.

But he wasn't going into battle. He was only trying to bond with his children. He'd tried to stay close to them the past four years, but his job had gotten in the way.

His job had been the cause for his divorce, too. At least that's what his wife had said. She'd thought marrying an FBI man would be romantic...until after the wedding. When she discovered that she'd spend a lot of time alone, she hadn't been so sure. But since she became pregnant with Cathy on the honeymoon, she'd put away her doubts.

Rob wasn't sure how Michael had happened. Another grin settled on his face as he considered that thought. He knew how Michael had happened, but neither he nor his wife had *intended* for Michael to happen.

In fact, when she discovered she was pregnant with Michael, his wife had confessed she'd already lined up the next husband. Though they'd stayed married until Michael's birth, the family had already failed.

When she'd called him last week to tell him she and her husband were moving to South America immediately, he'd been stunned. And angry. He didn't want his children so far away, where he wouldn't see them even as often as he did now. But the greatest surprise had been when his ex-wife had offered him custody of the children.

Without even thinking, his immediate response had been yes. He'd already lost so much of their childhood, and this would be his only chance to be a real father. He'd done a lot of good and helped a lot of people with his work, but he didn't hesitate to give it up. At once.

So last week he was deep undercover with a bunch of hoods, and this week he was planning his Thanksgiving dinner menu. Of course, they could have stayed in Kansas City, at his ex-wife's house, and had the Hutchinses prepare the feast, but he'd wanted the kids to himself. He'd wanted them to learn about his family.

He'd kept his grandparents' house as a fishing retreat and a home away from home, a safe house when his job got too hot. It had seemed the perfect place to bring Cathy and Michael.

Until Goldilocks showed up.

Already he knew he was attracted to the woman. Hell, what red-blooded male wouldn't be? But she had no place in their lives. He wasn't going to let lust mess up his chance to reclaim his family.

He decided the movie should be over by now. It was time to separate his children from Goldilocks.

The sight of the three of them snuggled together in his bed gave him pause. They looked as if they belonged together. Jessica noticed his arrival, but his children were too wrapped up in the story to pay him any attention.

He waited while Cinderella married her prince and they drove away in the elegant coach.

"Oh, that was wonderful!" Cathy said, clapping her hands together.

"Yes, I much prefer that fairy tale to The Three Bears," Jessica said, laughing. "Cinderella got to marry the handsome prince, and poor Goldilocks got scared to death and ran away. We don't even know if she got home all right."

"So you want to be married?" Rob asked. "Does that mean you're not married yet? I forgot to ask if there was an anxious husband at home."

"No! No, there's no anxious husband and no, I don't want to be married."

Her cheeks had actually paled, making him wonder about her response. "I didn't mean to upset you," he said softly.

Cathy got on her knees and patted Jessica's cheek. "Are you unhappy you don't have a prince?"

"It's just a fairy tale, Cathy," Jessica assured as she covered the child's little hand with her own. "Real life's not like a fairy tale. After all, you and Michael and your daddy aren't bears, are you? And you didn't chase me away. Instead you've fed me and made me feel welcome. That's better than the fairy tale, isn't it?''

"If the bears had known how nice Goldilocks was, I bet they wouldn't have chased her away,'' Cathy told her. "We like you.''

"Yeah!'' Michael agreed and began bouncing on the bed.

"Michael, I've told you my bed is not a trampoline. Hop off, and let's get you tucked into your own bed.'' Rob started toward his son, knowing from past experience how slowly Michael would follow that command.

"You tuck them in and I'll rewind the tape,'' Jessica offered.

"All right,'' Rob said. "Come on, Cathy, you, too. It's bedtime.''

"Can't Jessica come listen to our prayers, too, Daddy? Like a real family, a mommy and a daddy?'' Cathy asked, her gaze darting back and forth between the two adults.

Rob frowned, concerned that his little girl was spinning dreams about Jessica. After all, she would be gone tomorrow, he was sure, in spite of the snow that continued to cover the earth around them.

"I'd love to if you don't mind,'' Jessica said softly. She'd moved from the bed to stand beside it, Cathy's hand in hers.

"Of course I don't mind,'' Rob finally said. After all, what else could he say?

"Great. I'll start the tape rewinding.'' She moved

toward the television and Rob took Michael's hand and headed for the other room.

He'd put each child into the narrow bunk beds when Jessica appeared beside him in the almost dark room. He was seated on the edge of the bottom bunk, so she knelt down on the floor beside Michael's pillow.

"Am I too late? Have you already said your prayers?" she asked softly, smiling at Michael.

"No. I waited for you." He beamed at her and then very carefully folded his chubby little hands for prayer.

As his son recited, Rob wasn't surprised that Michael was charmed by Jessica. Even at four, the boy could recognize a beautiful woman. And a sweet one. Not too many women showed much attention to a little boy. Unless, of course, they were trying to charm his father. He looked sideways at her as Michael finished his prayer and she kissed his cheek.

"Ooh, you don't smell like Daddy," Michael said, reaching up to touch her soft cheek. "You don't feel like him, either."

"Um, well, no. I'm a girl, you know."

"You're like a real mommy, aren't you?"

"Michael—" Rob began, unsure what to say but certain he should steer his son's thoughts away from mommies.

"In some ways I am, because I'm a girl, but I'm not married and I don't have any children."

"Don't you want children?" Michael asked.

"Someday. Most ladies do, you know."

The problem for Rob had been that his wife didn't

want him, but at least she'd loved the kids. She'd cried when she'd told them goodbye. She hadn't cried when she'd told *him* to leave.

Again Jessica leaned down and kissed his son. "If I ever have children, I hope they're just like the two of you."

"Time to go to sleep, Michael," Rob said huskily. He bent over and kissed his son, too, tasting the lingering scent of Jessica's kiss, then drew the covers to Michael's chin and stood.

Jessica rose, too, and smiled at Cathy on the top bunk. "Have you already fallen asleep?"

"No, I waited," Cathy said. "I want a good-night kiss, too. I miss my mommy tucking me in."

Though Jessica shot him an alarmed look, she was sweetness itself to his little girl. "I'm happy to kiss you good-night, sweetheart. And I'm sure your mommy wishes she was here."

Rob snorted with laughter. She still thought he was an ax-murderer, he guessed. Kissing his daughter good-night, he escorted Jessica out of the bedroom.

In the hallway, Jessica suddenly seemed nervous. She avoided his gaze and then said hurriedly, "I'll go put the tape away. It should've finished rewinding by now."

He would've told her he could put the tape away later, but she'd already disappeared into his bedroom before he could speak. With a sigh, he followed her. His bedroom was the last place he wanted to see her.

With such thoughts in his head, it wasn't surprising that he scarcely paid attention to the television when he entered the room. The news was on, he realized, but he wasn't much interested in the doom and gloom they were offering tonight.

Jessica, however, was staring at it in horror.

"Jessica, is something wrong?"

She almost jumped out of her shoes. Immediately she ran to the television and slapped the Off button. She stood in front of it, as if shielding it from sight.

"No! No, nothing is wrong. Everything is fine. Just fine. The tape is rewound. Where shall I put it? Do you have the sleeve it goes in? Do you keep them in here? How many tapes do you have?"

He cut through her nervous chatter. "What are you trying to hide?"

"Hide? I don't know what you're talking about."

As a young man, he might've believed her denial. But as an ex-FBI agent and the seasoned father of two, he knew Jessica was lying. He reached around her and snapped on the television.

Chapter Four

The television, already warmed up from its earlier use, immediately showed a picture of a five-car pileup. He heard Jessica let out a deep sigh.

"They—they're having a lot of wrecks in Kansas City," she said, her words tripping over each other. "I can't bear to watch—I hate automobile accidents." She turned away from the television but carefully avoided his gaze.

"Now why don't I believe you?" he asked, studying her. "I think you're hiding something."

"Me? You're the one who says your ex-wife is in South America."

"Hey, that's the truth. Ask the kids." It amused him that she suspected him of something.

"They'll only repeat what you've told them."

"You're trying to distract me from whatever you saw on the news." He stared at the TV. "Did it have something to do with you?"

"Don't be ridiculous. What could I be hiding that would be on the news? Do you think I robbed a bank?"

With a grin, his gaze swept over her. "No, you're

not a bank robber. Maybe one of those ladies who go up to the hotel room with the traveling salesman, slip him a mickey and rob him? Yeah, I can see that. You've got the looks for that kind of job.''

She glared at him. ''Am I supposed to be flattered that I have the looks of a paid escort, a robber or a possible murderer? I don't think so!''

He pretended to reevaluate her looks, but he didn't need to look at her again. It probably wasn't wise to keep imprinting her on his brain…and other parts of his body. ''You're right. You're too classy to be an escort. A murderer, now…they come in all shapes and sizes…but probably not. Okay, so you tell me. What's your gig?''

''I *have* told you! I went for a drive and slid into a ditch because of the snow.''

Not quite an action that would make the news. But something on the television had shocked her—or scared her. The urge to pull her into his arms and soothe her fears needed to be squashed. Before he could stop himself, he'd taken a step toward her and reached out his hands.

When she moved back, he realized what he was doing and lowered his arms. ''What?'' he asked, hoping to cover his loss of control.

Her eyes widened as she met his gaze. ''What?''

''I asked first.''

''I don't know what you're asking.''

''You looked upset.'' He tried to read answers on her face.

She lowered her gaze, smoothing out her features.

"No, no, I'm just tired. It's not every day that I have this much excitement."

He'd forgotten all she'd been through—the accident, the struggle in the storm to find shelter, dealing with strangers. "Right, I'd forgotten." He looked over her shoulder at the big bed behind them. "That's the only other bed in the house. I don't guess you're willing to share?"

When her eyes widened with alarm, he hurriedly added, "I was just teasing, Jessica. I'll take the sofa downstairs." And forget those tempting visions of them sharing the bed where he'd discovered her earlier in the day, naked.

"I'll take the sofa."

"Nope, you stay here. After all, you're the guest." He reached out for her shoulders with the intention of shifting her to one side, but he snatched his fingers back after touching her. There was some sort of weird chemistry between them whenever he touched her.

Before he could move again, she spoke. "I'll take the sofa. I'm an uninvited guest at best. Besides, if the kids wake up during the night, they'll need you close."

"Damn. You're right." Two minutes with this lady and he was already forgetting about his kids' needs. That was why he had to get rid of Goldilocks right away. He wasn't going to mess up fatherhood again. Not when he'd been given a second chance. "It's just that they're not used to this place. Okay, you take the bathroom next, and I'll make up the sofa for you." He paused before asking, "Do you want a T-shirt to sleep in? I'm afraid that's all I have to offer.''

"That would be nice if you can spare one. I don't want to take over your entire wardrobe."

He grinned. "I have some old ones I leave here for extras. No problem."

Crossing the room, he pulled open a drawer and then tossed her a folded white T-shirt. "I'll be downstairs when you're finished." Downstairs and out of range of her particular allure.

AFTER ROB LEFT THE ROOM, Jessica sagged against the wall. A close call! When she'd come into the bedroom, the tape had already finished rewinding and a Kansas City news channel had filled the screen with her picture. Her father, not the police, was asking for information about her whereabouts. And he was offering a big reward.

While Rob didn't seem like a man who'd sell out his own mother, he might be interested in betraying a casual stranger. Especially for a big reward. She'd learned the hard way that money affected people strangely.

Jessica believed money had something to do with her engagement, too. She just didn't know how yet. But she didn't intend to let her father railroad her without finding out what was going on.

That's why she didn't want anyone to know where she was.

Her fingers caressed the T-shirt in her hands. Its softness brought her back to her situation. She was supposed to be preparing for bed. In the same house as the sexy man downstairs. The one she was tempted to touch every time he looked at her.

"This has got to stop!" she warned herself. Easier to say and do when he wasn't in the same room with her. With a sigh, she took the shirt and headed for the bathroom.

Five minutes later, having brushed her teeth with her finger and some toothpaste, exchanged the T-shirt for the sweatshirt and washed her face, she crept down the stairs. After the noisiness of the children, the silence unnerved her.

Before she'd gone too far, the ringing of the telephone interrupted the quiet. Somehow, it was encouraging to remember that they weren't completely cut off from the outside world. She heard Rob's deep voice answering.

"No! What are you doing calling me now?"

He didn't seem too pleased. She knew she shouldn't eavesdrop, but she couldn't help it. He was speaking loudly.

"No!" He exploded again. "I won't do it." Silence. "I don't care what you threaten to do. Just leave me alone!"

She was halfway down the stairs and growing concerned about what she was hearing. She shifted over several steps so she could see Rob standing by the phone, talking.

"I've had enough of the nastiness, the...the horror. I don't want to be a part of it anymore. I explained that."

The nastiness? The horror? What was he talking about?

"No, I won't. I gave you everything I had so you could continue. That's it. I'm going to spend my time being a daddy."

She appreciated his good intentions, but could he walk away from whatever horrible thing he was involved with?

"Don't threaten me, Sims! And don't even think about talking to my kids." He slammed the phone down and began pacing the room, running his fingers through his thick, dark hair.

She couldn't resist. Hurrying down the last of the stairs, she stepped into the den. "And you think I have something to hide? At least I'm not being chased by—" she halted, suddenly wondering if she could honestly make that statement. After all, it was her picture, not his, that was on the news.

"I mean, no one's threatening—" Oops! Her father had threatened, but not like—well, she didn't know exactly what Sims had threatened.

"I mean, you're the one with something to hide, not me!" she finally finished saying.

"And you have nothing to hide?" he asked, returning her attack.

Why did she have to be so honest? "Well, nothing bad like you. No wonder you're hiding here. You've put your children's lives in danger!" She gasped. "And mine, too, I guess. What's going to happen to us?"

"You're being neurotic. Nothing is going to happen to my children...or you. No one's coming here to threaten any of you, so just forget you ever heard that conversation and go to sleep."

"You're treating me like a child. Do you think it's easy to forget that someone or something nasty and horrible is threatening us?"

"How much did you hear?" he demanded, stepping toward her.

With the conversation on her mind, it wasn't a giant leap to realize she might be in as much danger from the handsome man in front of her as from anyone else. She put the sofa between them.

"All—all of it."

"Well, forget all of it, okay? It has nothing to do with you. Or my kids."

She was distracted from his words as he moved around the sofa toward her. Panicked, she tried to run, but he reached out a long arm to stop her. His pull unbalanced her and she flopped over the back of the sofa as if she were a wounded duck.

Since the seat was soft, her fall wasn't a problem. Until he landed on top of her.

Too stunned to react, Jessica stared into his eyes, mesmerized by the feel of him against her. All her earlier attraction, denied but not forgotten, surged through her. She felt her body melting, drawing his weight into her. The reaction scared her. She knew she had to protest at once before it was too late.

"*Aghhh!*" she screamed before a big hand clapped down over her mouth.

"You're going to wake the kids!" he warned.

As if that should be her major concern. She squirmed against him, pushing to be released, her eyes wide with apprehension of her own reaction as much as his. She might have fantasized about sharing a bed with him, but she didn't intend to let it happen.

"Would you stop moving? You're going to cause more trouble than you— Damn it, Jess—" He closed his eyes and rolled off of her to the floor. It didn't take long to figure out what he meant. She already knew how her own body was responding to him.

And she wasn't talking about fear.

Before she could protest, he rolled to his feet and strode to the door. She thought he was going to leave without speaking, but he halted, clutching the doorjamb, keeping his back to her.

"Forget the conversation you heard, okay? You're safe. At least you will be as soon as I get up those stairs. I'll see you in the morning."

ROB RUBBED THE GRIT from his eyes. They felt as if they'd been sandpapered. But he knew better. The discomfort was caused by lack of sleep. After lying on top of Jessica for thirty seconds last night, he'd spent hours telling his body no dice.

It hadn't liked his orders.

After he washed his hands, he opened the refrigerator and pulled out the big turkey he'd bought yesterday. He eyed it uneasily. Maybe he'd been more ambitious than he was wise.

No. He was going to make the first Thanksgiving he'd ever shared with his children a good one. That's why he'd crawled out of bed at six in the morning to cook a humongous bird.

He ripped the plastic off the turkey and shuddered

as his fingers came into contact with clammy flesh. *Ugh!* Not like Jessica's skin...silky, warm, enticing. *Enough!* He didn't need to think about last night, that brief time when she'd been snug beneath his body, when he'd realized her breasts were free under that soft T-shirt.

He shook his head and tried to remember what Mrs. H. had told him. Oh, yeah. Stick his hand inside and bring out the package of gizzards. That ought to take his mind off the beautiful Goldilocks sleeping a few feet away from him.

"What are you doing?"

The unexpected sound of Jessica's throaty voice caused Rob to lose his hold on the damn turkey and it bounced off the edge of the counter onto the floor, landing with a big splat.

"Look what you did!" he yelled.

"Me? I didn't do anything!"

Then he took stock of her appearance and groaned. "Where are those sweatpants?"

Her gaze reflected her confusion as she stared first at her bare legs and then at him. "What?"

How could he explain that the sight of her long, bare legs, beneath the hem of his T-shirt, reaching to midthigh, was more stimulation than he needed, especially after last night.

"Never mind." He bent down and picked up the turkey. "Do you think it'll be all right if I wash it?"

"With soap?"

He turned to stare at her. "You think I should use soap?"

"I don't know. I don't know anything about cooking, remember?"

"If we were going to have unexpected company," he grumbled, "why couldn't it have been Martha Stewart?"

She folded her arms across her chest, drawing attention to a part of her anatomy he was trying to ignore. "Thanks for making me feel welcome."

"I'm sorry, Jess, I didn't mean—" He found himself talking to emptiness as the kitchen door swung slowly back and forth, emphasizing her exit.

"Damn, damn, damn!" He and his big mouth. Why couldn't he have kept it shut? Now he had a bruised, dirty turkey and an angry houseguest. And it was only six in the morning. At this rate, Thanksgiving dinner would be a complete disaster.

JESSICA STOMPED back into the den where she'd tossed and turned all night to find the highly valued sweatpants. At least by her host. She would've put them on before venturing to the kitchen if she'd thought she would encounter Rob. But she'd heard something and remnants of the conversation she'd overheard last night had her leaping to conclusions.

Clutching the sweatpants to her chest, she scurried up the stairs after a cautious look toward the kitchen door. Her clothes would be dry, and she intended to don them at once. That way the bear downstairs would have no cause for complaints.

She entered the bedroom and came to a halt, staring at the big bed, the covers twisted into a misshapen pile. Someone else had had a restless night.

Ah, well, misery loved company. At least she knew she wasn't the only one to suffer.

Wiping the smile of satisfaction off her face before anyone could see it, she gathered her clothes and headed for the bathroom. The sooner she was dressed in *her* clothes, the sooner she would feel in control.

When she returned to the kitchen a few minutes later, desperately in search of caffeine in the form of coffee, she discovered Rob in much the same position as before.

"I hesitate to say anything in case I'm blamed for World War III, but I'll ask again. What are you doing?"

This time he kept hold of the turkey, only turning his head. "I'm trying to get this turkey ready to go in the oven."

"Did you wash it?"

"Yes. I didn't use soap, but I scrubbed it real good."

She tiptoed over to the sink, and when she reached Rob's side, she peered over his muscled arms and frowned. "Why do you have your hand stuck in the turkey?"

"It's a new kind of winter glove. Chic, isn't it?" he drawled and glared at her.

His mood clearly hadn't improved since she'd left the kitchen. She took a step back.

As if her withdrawal triggered his conscience, he muttered, "I'm sorry. And I'm sorry for what I said earlier. I'm like a fish out of water here, and I wanted to make Thanksgiving special for my children.''

"Well, I'm no Martha Stewart," she said, deliberately using his own words to show she'd forgiven him, "but I'll do anything I can to help."

"Anything?"

Misgiving filled her, but she staunchly repeated her offer. "Anything."

Instead of answering, he tugged his hand out of the turkey. "Stick your hand in there and pull out the gizzards."

Her eyes widened and she wondered if it was too late to take back her offer. But the look in his eyes told her he expected her to refuse. Her chin rose. She wasn't going to be defeated by a macho man and a dead bird.

"Should I wash my hands first?"

"Uh, yeah." He shifted over a little more, but she had to stand right next to him, almost touching his strong thighs, feeling his breath on her cheek as she washed her hands.

"Okay," she said, drawing a deep breath, hoping her hands wouldn't shake. "I just stick my hand in that hole?"

"Yep. According to Mrs. H., our housekeeper, there's supposed to be a packet of gizzards inside the bird."

She breathed a sigh of relief. "Oh. It's in a package, like a sack?"

"Well, sure. Did you think you were just going to yank the insides out?" The twinkle in his eye told her he was laughing at her.

"Would you know any different if your house-keeper hadn't told you?" she challenged.

He had the grace to smile, acknowledging a hit. "Nope."

With a determined nod, she slowly slid her hand into the hole. "Couldn't you find it?"

"I couldn't even get my damn hand in the hole. It's too small. That's why I thought maybe you could help. You're a little more petite than me."

She couldn't hold back a giggle. "I don't think petite would be a word anyone would ever associate with you."

"Dainty?" he offered, grinning.

"Hardly. Surly, grouchy, big, maybe, but not dainty."

"Well, now, sweetheart—" he began, still smiling.

"I got it!" Jessica shrieked, beaming as she pulled the small packet of turkey innards out of the fowl and held it up above her head.

"Congratulations!" Rob responded, a big smile on his face, as if she'd accomplished some impossible goal.

Before Jessica realized what was going on, his arms surrounded her and he lifted her up into the air. Then, as he slowly slid her down his big, muscular body, the smiles disappeared and the turkey was forgotten.

His arms held her tightly against him, and her body responded to his as it had last night. But this time, he didn't roll away. This time, he pressed even tighter. With even greater results.

Jessica felt her body come to attention, as if responding to a summons or an electrical charge. Her breasts tightened and her nipples pushed against his chest. As her breath quickened, her lids drifted down over her eyes.

"Jess..." he muttered and buried his face against her neck.

Confused, sure he'd been about to kiss her, she opened her mouth to protest, but he lifted his head and changed directions, settling his warm lips over hers. With a shudder of desire, she surrendered to his touch.

Until he jerked away.

"What's wrong?" she asked, her gaze fixed on his lips. Those wonderful, magical lips.

"You just dropped a slimy sack of turkey gizzards down my back."

Chapter Five

Rob figured he'd have to add a special thanks for turkey gizzards in his prayers. Otherwise, he'd have made love to Jessica on the kitchen floor.

Her cheeks were red with embarrassment, as if the kiss had been her fault. He wanted to reassure her, but how could he do that without confessing how much he wanted her?

"Turn around and I'll get it out," she mumbled, still not looking at him.

He did as she asked and then had to suffer through her pulling his shirt out from his jeans. Fortunately, once the shirt was free, the sack fell to the floor and she didn't have to touch his skin. He picked up the packet and tossed it into the sink.

"Your shirt is all wet. Maybe you'd better go change."

"Okay. I guess the turkey can wait another couple of minutes. Anything you can do to help would be appreciated." Without looking at her, he raced out the door and up the stairs.

JESSICA STARED at the raw turkey, wondering what one was supposed to *do* to it. After her mother's

death, she and her father had taken most of their
Thanksgiving meals at the country club. After all,
the staff deserved a day off occasionally. She studied the turkey from one side and then the other, but
no inspiration hit her.

Then the phone rang.

Immediately she remembered the conversation
she'd overheard last night. Which meant she
shouldn't answer the phone.

She moved to the hallway and stared upstairs.
Rob's bedroom door was closed. He probably
couldn't hear the phone ringing.

Curiosity killed the cat. But she wasn't a cat. With
another look upstairs, she hurried into the den and
picked up the phone.

"Hello?"

Silence.

She repeated her breathless greeting.

"Is Rob there?"

"Yes, he's upstairs. Shall I call him to the
phone?"

"Yes."

That's all the gruff voice said. Darn. She'd hoped
for more information. But maybe the caller wasn't
the same as last night. She laid down the phone and
hurried up the stairs. If she called out, she'd wake
the children.

Knocking, she leaned closer to the door and whispered, "Rob?"

The door opened and she discovered Rob with his
jeans unzipped as he stuffed in his shirt. It wasn't

as if she could see any skin, she reminded herself as her cheeks warmed.

"Uh, sorry, but there's a phone call for you."

"You answered the phone?" he demanded, frowning.

"It might have woken the kids if I hadn't," she assured him with self-righteousness. Besides driving her crazy with curiosity.

"Who is it?"

"I don't know. He didn't say."

Rob zipped up his jeans as he moved past her, and she let her imagination escape, picturing a different outcome to his undressed state. She almost forgot the phone call with her thoughts.

Until she heard Rob's irritated voice answering the phone. Then she hurried down the stairs after him.

"Do you have any idea what time it is here?"

She did. Six-thirty. Too early for everything that had already happened.

"It's Thanksgiving!"

Right again. So far she wasn't learning anything new.

"No! I told you last night."

Aha! At least she'd discovered one thing. It was Sims on the phone.

Rob was pacing back and forth, the phone in his hand as he listened to what a suddenly long-winded Sims had to say. Jessica began to worry that whatever the man had in mind, he'd convince Rob to join in.

Rob let out a gusty sigh and ran his fingers

through his thick hair. "Look, I— Okay, I'll do that much. I've got a couple of ideas that should create some mayhem. Let me do some more thinking and I'll call you Monday. I should be back in Kansas City by then."

Jessica's heart double-clutched. *No! Don't return to a life of crime!* Planning was as good as doing in the eyes of the law. She didn't want to see Rob behind bars. What would happen to his children?

Somehow, until now, she hadn't pictured him as a criminal. His easygoing smile, the tenderness he showed his children, even his gentlemanly resistance to her, damn his hide, didn't make him appear a criminal. But now she had proof from his own mouth that he would do something bad. Mayhem had to be bad.

"You'll just have to wait, Sims. I'm going to enjoy Thanksgiving with my children." He slammed down the receiver, not giving Sims time to respond.

Then he looked up and saw her.

"It's not nice to listen in on other people's conversations." Without waiting for her to apologize, if she was going to, he headed for the kitchen.

She followed him and watched silently as he placed the turkey in a large pan.

"I don't think you should."

He looked over his shoulder, a salt shaker in his hand. "Mrs. H. said to salt it on the inside."

"Not that. What—what you said on the phone."

He rolled his eyes and turned back to the turkey. Standing the bird on its neck, he shook salt through the hole she'd earlier become familiar with.

"Rob! Don't ignore me. You've got your children to think of."

"I *am* thinking of my children. And I don't need your advice." He put the turkey in the big pan and covered it with the matching lid, then carried it over to the oven. "Damn, I forgot to move the shelf down. Would you get a hot pad and shift it to the bottom?"

She did as he asked, but she wasn't giving up their conversation. "I think you're being rude."

"Hell, lady, if moving a shelf is too much to ask, leave the kitchen!"

"You know that's not what I'm talking about! Of course it isn't too much trouble. There! Now there's room for the stupid turkey."

He slid the big pan inside, closed the door and turned to grin at her. "You require a smart turkey for dinner? What IQ is necessary before you can eat?"

"You're being ridiculous! I'm trying to save you!"

"From what? Eating the wrong turkey? It's the only one we have and I intend to chow down about two o'clock. But don't worry. If you've become a vegetarian after wrestling with its insides, there'll be potatoes, English peas and carrots to go with it."

Frustration welled up in her. She didn't want to know why saving this man from a life of crime was so important to her. She just knew it was. "Rob, I'm talking about what you promised Sims!"

"Sims! How do you know his name? He didn't give it to you, did he?"

"No. You called him that several times."

"I told you to forget those calls. Do you hear me?"

She reached out to touch his arm as they stood by the oven. He jerked away as if she'd burned him. "Rob, even if you don't do anything, you'll be guilty for planning it. Don't let the man persuade you to get involved."

His eyes darkened and one brow slid up. "You're worried about me?"

There was heat in his look, heat that she craved and yet knew she couldn't give in to. After all, she had just broken her engagement. And he was probably a criminal. But it was hard to back away, especially after that earlier kiss.

"Of course I am. For the children's sake."

He grinned and she was afraid she was going to melt.

"My children are safe. And we're going to have turkey for Thanksgiving." He stepped away from her. "Now, I'm going to try for a nap before those children you're so worried about wake up. Because once they do, no one will get any rest."

He walked out of the kitchen, saving her from throwing herself into his arms. Not that she really would have, of course. She wasn't that kind of woman.

At least she hadn't been that kind of woman with Stephen. He'd pressed her to become more intimate, but she'd told him she wanted to wait. But with Rob... All he had to do was enter a room, and she was filled with desire.

With a sigh, she headed back to the sofa. A nap sounded like a good idea. Otherwise, she might march up those stairs and find satisfaction with a criminal!

ROB LED HIS TROOPS down the stairs on tiptoe.

"Shh! Go in the kitchen. I'll be right there." He watched, his hands on his hips, as his children quietly followed his orders. They were good kids. He was a lucky man. Even luckier because he had Goldilocks sleeping in the den. Or unlucky. She was a big temptation. He'd run away earlier, because if he hadn't gotten out of there fast, he would've grabbed her again. And they didn't have the turkey gizzards to rescue them this time.

Once the kitchen door was closed, he moved into the den and stared at Jessica. She was curled up under the quilt, her eyes closed, her long brown lashes resting against her soft skin. Man, she was a beauty. Maybe after he got his kids settled in, he could look her up.

He realized he didn't even know where she lived. Or anything else about her except her name. Suddenly he remembered her accusations last night after his phone conversation with Sims. She'd accused him of being chased...and stopped. Then she'd accused him of being threatened...and stopped again. And she hadn't been able to deny that she was hiding something.

Was she the one in trouble instead of him?

The urge to protect her surged through him. And why not? She was as naive as his children, trusting a stranger as she had. Hell, she'd done more than trust him. She'd let him kiss the daylights out of her. If he hadn't called a halt—he'd better not think about that again.

He quietly left the den. She might as well sleep while she could. And his kids were waiting for breakfast. His kids were top priority, not a sexy Goldilocks. He'd best remember that.

JESSICA STRETCHED and yawned simultaneously until her elbow collided with the back of the sofa. Then she remembered she wasn't in her luxurious bedroom. She was hiding in a cabin in the woods with the Berensons. Or, as Cathy liked to think, the three bears.

Certainly one of them was a bear. Rob growled at her frequently, particularly when she listened to his phone conversations. She sat up abruptly, thinking about their argument over his planned mayhem.

Urgency filled her. She had to convince Rob to avoid any association with the dastardly Sims. Since she'd gone to sleep fully clothed, she quickly folded the quilt and then hurried to the kitchen.

Two things stopped her from immediately introducing the topic at hand. Cathy and Michael. They were "helping" their father cook. At least Jessica thought that was what they were doing.

"How much do I put in, Daddy?" Cathy asked.

"All of it, Cathy— No, Michael! Not yet!"

"Something smells good," Jessica said, smiling at the trio. Michael was sitting on the cabinet and Cathy was standing on a chair beside her father.

"Oh, you're awake," Rob said, but his gaze was much more intensive than his mild comment.

"Don't sound so welcoming, Papa Bear," she replied.

Both children laughed.

Rob glared.

"Have I overslept the Thanksgiving feast?" she asked Cathy, ignoring Rob.

"No, the turkey is still cooking. We're making stuffing."

"Really? I'm impressed."

Rob seemed to have gotten over his irritation. "Don't be. It's from a box."

"Ah. For a minute there, I thought I was going to have to feel greatly inferior to you." He grinned at her teasing and she smiled back, feeling welcome again. "Is there anything I can do to help?"

"Are you any good at slicing carrots?"

"I've never tried, but I'm willing to give it a go."

He gave her a few directions and then returned to the stuffing. As soon as he put it in the oven, he sent the children upstairs to watch the Thanksgiving Day parade on television, promising to call them before he took the turkey from the oven.

Jessica had been slowly working on the carrots, fearing they looked more like totem poles than carrots by the time she'd cleaned them. Then, with a sharp knife, she had laid them on a chopping board and set to slicing them.

She was so involved in her unusual task that she didn't notice the children's disappearance until Rob paused beside her and asked in a low voice, "Who's chasing you?"

With a gasp, she hit the carrot under her knife so hard, half of it went flying through the air. "What are you doing?" she demanded. "You scared me to death. I have a knife."

He backed a foot away, his hands extended, palms out. "Hey, I asked a question. Don't threaten me."

She looked down at the knife she now had pointed at Rob's stomach. Carefully laying it down on the chopping board, she faced him again. "I wasn't threatening you. You surprised me, that's all."

"Whew, thank goodness. I was beginning to think you were the ax-murderer, not me."

"I told you I haven't killed anyone, which is more than you've done. Can you tell me you haven't killed a person, particularly your wife?"

"I haven't killed my *ex*-wife," he said solemnly, lifting only one hand this time.

She narrowed her gaze. His response had been very specific. "Can you promise you haven't killed *anyone?*" Her heart contracted as he lowered his hand, frowning. "Rob?"

"Honey, I can't—there are some things I can't tell you about, but I've never hurt anyone unless I had to."

She took a step back. "What—what do you mean?"

He reached out and grabbed her by the waist, pulling her against him. "Come on, now, Jess, don't be silly. I'm not going to hurt you. You know that, don't you?"

Slowly she nodded her head. As much as it went against logic, she knew she was safe with him. Maybe too safe.

"Besides, you're the one with the knife, not me."

The warmth of his body was enveloping her, and she knew she needed to put some distance between them if she was going to keep her resistance strong. Reaching for the knife, she broke his hold on her. "I have to get back to work. I'm slow since I haven't done this before."

"Okay, we'll talk while you work."

She eyed him suspiciously. "You haven't been very chatty before. What do you want to talk about?"

"We could start with you answering my question."

"What question is that?" she asked, stalling for time.

"Who's chasing you? That's the question."

"Why would you ask that?"

He reached up and smoothed a strand of hair behind her ear. "Curiosity?"

She hacked a chunk off the end of the carrot she was holding. "That's a silly question. Who would be chasing me?"

"That was my question."

"Is this too big?" she asked, holding up the chunk she'd just cut.

"Of course not, if a giant was eating with us. The pieces are supposed to be bite-size...I think."

"This is a case of the blind leading the blind,"

she muttered and concentrated on cutting the chunk into two pieces. "There. That's better, isn't it?"

"Yeah, great. Would you answer the question?"

"I don't know why you would bother me with such a silly question. I'm trying to help cook Thanksgiving dinner...without a lot of appreciation, I might add."

"Sweetheart, I recognize a stall when I see one. I've had a lot of experience in questioning—I mean—"

"Yes? A lot of experience in what? You never said what kind of work you do. Do you torture people for the Mob?"

"No! I mean, not unless—wait a minute. I'm the one asking questions."

"Not unless what?" Fear was building in her. Not fear that he would hurt her, but fear that he might already have committed crimes. That he might go to prison no matter how good he was to his children. No matter how nice he had been to her. No matter if someone cared about him.

"Jess, I'm trying to find out if you're in trouble. Do you need help?"

"Me? Of course not. What makes you think—"

"Last night, you said—that is, you tried to say no one was chasing you, but you stopped. Then you said no one was threatening you, but you stopped. I would've picked up on it then, but we got distracted."

Her face burned as she remembered the momentary distraction. Thirty seconds had never loomed larger in her life. "It wasn't my fault. If you hadn't chased me and—and fallen—"

"I know, I know."

She turned her attention back to the carrots. He took the knife from her hand.

"Come on, Jess, tell me the truth."

"The truth is I don't need any help." She looked him right in the eye, knowing her response was honest. Someone was chasing her, threatening her, and she had something to hide. But she would deal with her problems alone.

He stared at her, his hazel eyes puzzled, but she didn't look away. Honesty was a great weapon. "Okay," he said with a sigh.

"May I have the knife back, please, so I can finish this chore?"

"All right, but let me show you how to cut them. It'll be faster." Instead of handing her the knife, he moved behind her and encircled her with his arms. Placing one hand on hers holding a carrot, he put the knife in her other hand and wrapped his hand around hers. She was completely surrounded with the warmth of Rob Berenson.

"See? You chop along the carrot until you reach the end. Just be sure you get your fingers out of the way before you get there."

It was hard to remember such unimportant items as fingers or carrots or dinner or even her father and Stephen as long as she was so close to Rob. Her breathing grew shallow and her body tightened. "I—I can—"

Before she could finish her assertion, he'd put

down the knife and turned her in his arms. He forgot the carrots, too, as his lips settled over hers and he pulled her closer. Her hands slid around his neck and she matched his eagerness. Rob's lips taught her the difference between a kiss and the meeting of two souls thirsting for each other. The difference between a spring rain and Noah's forty days and forty nights. The difference between friendliness and true love.

The shock of that thought blasted through her daze and she jerked back from Rob's hold. "No!"

Rob still seemed to be under the power of their embrace as he muttered, "Yes," and sought her lips again.

But Jessica feared the enemy within. She knew she shouldn't love Rob. He might be a criminal. He probably would be interested in her money. And he definitely wouldn't be interested in anything permanent.

"No," she said again, and ran from the kitchen.

Chapter Six

Rob took out his frustration, of which he had a considerable amount, on the carrots. They may have been more finely chopped than was warranted, but he felt better by the time he put them on the stove to cook.

It looked as if he'd have to finish cooking by himself, unless he wanted to summon his children. But he thought the task would be easier alone. It would give him time to think, too. Normally he had great control. Working undercover the past few years, his life had depended on his self-control.

So what was wrong now? Why did he forget to keep his distance every time Jessica came near him? The last thing he needed right now was a woman in his life. He was going to have to put all his energy into learning to be a father.

He opened several cans of English peas and poured them into a pan, adding a dash of salt. All he had left to prepare were the rolls. As he set them on a cookie sheet and added a bit of margarine on each one, his mind wandered back to Jessica.

Could he believe her when she said she wasn't in

trouble? He'd sensed honesty in her words. She'd promised she didn't— Wait a minute! She hadn't said she wasn't in trouble. She'd said she didn't need any help.

His eyes narrowed as he stared across the kitchen, trying to remember her exact words.

Yes, that's what she'd said. Did that mean she really was in trouble? He finally shrugged his shoulders in frustration. How could he know if she wouldn't confide in him? And since he'd known her less than twenty-four hours, even he wouldn't advise her to trust a stranger.

He concentrated on Thanksgiving dinner after that conclusion. Finally, with the table set and the turkey nicely browned and sitting in the center of the table, he put the rolls into the oven and headed upstairs to see where his dinner guests were.

"Hi, Daddy!" Michael called as Rob stopped in the doorway to his bedroom where the television was located. Cathy distractedly echoed Michael's greeting.

"Ready to eat, guys? Go wash up before the turkey gets cold."

The two children slid down from the bed.

"Have you seen Jessica?" he asked. He'd already checked the downstairs rooms and hadn't found her. Had she disappeared as abruptly as she'd come into their lives?

"No. Did we lose her?" Cathy asked, frowning anxiously.

"I'm sure we didn't. Maybe she's taking a nap in

your room. I'll check while you're in the bathroom.''

When he opened the door to the second bedroom,
he breathed a sigh of relief when he saw her standing by the window, staring out at the snow. Not that
it mattered to him that she share Thanksgiving dinner with him and his children. He just didn't want
her lost in the snowstorm.

"Hungry?" he asked softly.

She started and then drew a deep breath before
she turned around to face him. "Yes, I am. I hope
you'll let me eat after deserting you in the kitchen.''

Her facing up to what had happened between
them surprised and pleased him. "I think maybe you
had good reason to leave. I apologize."

"That's not necessary," she said briskly. "We'll
just forget it ever happened."

He doubted his ability to do that, but he appreciated her attitude. His ex-wife had sulked and
pouted forever when something displeased her.

"Where are the children?"

"They're washing up now. The three of you can
come down as soon as you're ready."

Her smile wasn't the room brightener he'd seen
earlier, but at least it was a smile. He ran down the
stairs, his heart feeling lighter, prepared to celebrate
Thanksgiving with his children and a bewitching
woman.

A few minutes later, after a Thanksgiving prayer
had been given, Rob carved the turkey while the
others passed around the side dishes.

"Everything looks lovely, Rob," Jessica said. "I'm impressed."

"Yeah, Daddy, this looks almost as good as Nana's dinners."

"Almost?" he objected, but he smiled at his daughter to let her know he was teasing.

"I want a drumstick," Michael announced, not interested in the niceties. As always, he seemed to be thinking of his stomach.

Jessica lifted her head and sniffed the air.

"Is something burning?"

Rob leaped up from the table. "Damn! The rolls!" He saw Cathy cover her mouth with one hand, indicative of his curse, but he'd have to worry about that later. Grabbing a hot pad, he yanked open the oven door and pulled out a cookie sheet of very brown rolls.

He turned around to his audience with a wry grimace. "Looks like we're having burned rolls for dinner."

"Not burned, just crispy. That's just how I like my bread," Jessica assured him. "Right, kids?"

"Right, Daddy," Cathy said. "They make the butter melt good."

"I want one," Michael called out.

"Thanks, guys." Rob felt grateful for their generosity. He slid the rolls onto a plate and brought them to the table. When he settled back down in his chair, he leaned over to Cathy. "I know I shouldn't have said that word. Will you forgive me?"

"Sure, Daddy." She gave him a bright smile, one that reminded him again of how lucky he was.

Everything was perfect—except for the overdone rolls—for their dinner together. Rob was congratulating himself when he saw Jessica's eyes widen.

"Quick, duck! Under the table!"

He stared at her and then at his children as they followed her directions at once.

"Rob!" she called, her voice muffled.

He lifted the tablecloth and looked under the table to find three faces watching him. "Is this a new game I don't know about?"

"I don't know, Daddy, but it's fun," Cathy assured him.

"It's no game! It's Sims!" Jessica assured him hoarsely, her eyes still wide with what he finally recognized as fear.

"What are you talking about?" But before she could answer, there was a knock at the door.

"Don't answer it!" she pleaded.

"Everyone sit back up. This is not Sims, Jessica. He couldn't get here this fast if he tried. And he's not trying, I can assure you." By the time he finished speaking, his companions were once again visible above the table. Another knock sounded at the door.

"Wait here."

He went to the front door. Who would be out in this snowstorm? True, it wasn't snowing nearly as hard as it had been earlier, but the roads would still be impassable. He opened the door and discovered two young men in ski clothes with poles and cross-country skis.

"Uh, hi, we've been skiing and—and we wondered if we could come in and get warm before we start back," one man said. "We kinda went farther than we intended."

They appeared harmless enough. Rob backed up, opening the door to them. "Sure, come on in."

"We'll leave our skis out here, so we won't track up your house. I hope I didn't scare anyone when I looked in your window. We didn't think anyone lived out here," the second young man said.

Ah. His face in the window must be what had made Jessica react so strangely. Though why she should think it would be Sims, he didn't know. She must be more worried about his phone calls than he'd realized.

"No, not at all," he lied. "We've just finished dinner and have plenty left. Would you care to eat?"

The two young men reminded him of Michael at the mention of food. "Wow, that'd be great," the first man said.

Rob led the way to the kitchen. "We've got some cold and hungry skiers, guys. Can we make room for them at the table?" He smiled at Jessica, hoping to relieve her anxieties.

While he rounded up two more chairs, Jessica got a couple of clean plates and silverware and brought them to the table without saying anything.

"You were playing in the snow?" Michael asked.

Rob could read his son's mind. "Don't even think about it, Michael. You're not going outside to play until the snow stops."

"Aw, Daddy," Michael protested.

"We weren't playing," the first guy said. "We

were cross-country skiing, and we went farther than we meant to.''

Rob began carving more turkey. ''I suppose we should introduce ourselves. I'm Rob. This is Jessica, Cathy and Michael,'' he added, nodding his head to each as he introduced them.

''We're Jason and Duane. We live in Jackson.''

''You skied from there?'' Rob asked in surprise.

''Sort of. I live on a farm a couple of miles from town. Really, we're a little lost,'' Jason added.

''I can point you in the right direction after you've eaten,'' Rob assured him. He looked over at Duane, who was giving all his attention to Jessica, a puzzled expression on his face.

''Don't I know you from somewhere?'' the young man finally asked her.

Her face paled and Rob was afraid she was going to pass out.

''No!'' Jessica snapped and looked away from the young man.

''Are you sure?''

''We've never met,'' she assured him firmly. ''Would you like some carrots?'' Her attempt to distract him was fairly obvious.

''Yes, thank you,'' he replied politely. However, the carrots didn't sidetrack him. ''I know we've never met, but are you someone famous?''

''She's Jessica,'' Cathy said, watching the exchange.

The young man grinned. ''Yeah, but she looks

familiar to me. Are you one of those reporters on
television? Or an anchorwoman?''

"No, I'm in accounting," she said briefly. One·
quick glance at Rob and she looked down at her
plate. He had turned a speculative gaze on her also.

Jason, the other young man, grinned and muttered, "I've never seen an accountant who looked
like you.''

She glared at him and then shared her displeasure
with Rob as he chuckled.

"I know what you mean," Rob said to Jason,
who was embarrassed by his words. "Jessica is shy.
She's not really mad at you. Right, Jessica?''

With a sigh, she assured the boy she wasn't angry.
In fact, she was more perturbed by Duane's continued staring. She was afraid he'd seen her picture on
the news last night. With the hope of taking his·
thoughts away from her identity, she began asking
them questions about school and their families, de-
terminedly keeping the conversation away from her
while they ate.

When the boys had finished, Rob brought out a
coconut cake and a pumpkin pie for dessert.

"I'm really impressed," Jessica said, surprised.

"Don't be. Mrs. H. made these for me before we
left Kansas City. But I'm prepared to spray whipped
cream on everyone's piece of pie. I'm sure I'll show
real artistic talent when I do that.''

Jessica returned his grin. He had a great sense of
humor. "Then I'll have pumpkin pie. I can't wait to
see you at work.''

"Me, too, Daddy," Cathy said, siding with Jessica, as usual.

They ate their dessert quietly, Jessica having run out of questions. In fact, she was worrying about when the two boys would leave. It would get dark early, what with the snow and the time of the year. She didn't want these two staying the night.

"We'd better be on our way," Jason finally said after his second piece of cake. "We sure appreciate the meal and letting us warm up." He pushed back his chair and stood, but Duane didn't move.

"Come on, Duane. We've got to go."

Jessica kept her gaze on her pumpkin pie, holding her breath for Duane's response.

"I don't think we can get back before dark."

"We'd better or both our dads will ground us for sure. You remember what they said before we took off," Jason warned.

"Sounds like my dad," Rob said with a smile. "And that means you'd better be on your way. I have a compass you can take with you. You'll get back faster if you stay on track. We're almost directly southwest from town."

Jessica breathed a sigh of relief as the two boys headed for the door, Rob following. Just as they pushed the door open, however, Duane came to an abrupt halt. "Wait! I know who you are!"

In the tense silence that followed his exclamation, Cathy was the first to speak. "She's Jessica," she explained again, a puzzled sound in her voice.

"Yeah! Jessica Barnes!" Duane responded.

"And?" Rob questioned.

"You know, the one on the news last night. I don't usually watch it, but I wanted to know if it was going to keep snowing and—"

"I think you'd better be going before it gets dark," Jessica said. She walked toward the door to usher them out.

"So I guess someone's already collected the reward? Man, it was a big one. What I couldn't do with that money." Duane shrugged. "Didn't your dad know where you were going for Thanksgiving?"

As if he had the right to her innermost secrets, Jessica thought in irritation. "It was a misunderstanding, that's all. My father is overly protective."

"Too bad I didn't know where you were last night. I'd have me a Harley today if I had."

Jessica tried to smile, but she wasn't sure it was successful. How easy in a teenager's mind to give a little information and get a lot of cash. What did it matter that he would be creating all kinds of problems for her?

"That's life," Rob assured him, slapping him on the shoulder as he encouraged them on their way.

As the three males left the room, she organized the kids to help her clean the table. Cathy, carrying several glasses to the sink where Jessica had run hot water to wash, asked, "What did that boy mean?"

"About what, sweetie?"

Before Cathy could explain, Rob returned. "Upstairs, kids. There's a special on television."

Though Cathy's face showed reluctance, she

knew better than to argue with her father when he used that tone of voice.

It didn't take an Einstein for Jessica to guess Rob wanted to question her and she couldn't think of any way to avoid his interrogation.

Once the door closed behind the children, Rob came over to the sink where she'd begun to wash the dishes. "Well?"

"I'm washing, so you have to dry after you rinse. Spread a tea towel on the cabinet so the dishes can drain."

"You know that's not what I'm asking. What Duane said was why you shut off the television last night, wasn't it?"

"Yes." She thoroughly scrubbed a plate, refusing to look at him.

"Why? I thought you called your father."

"Yes, but it was too late to take the request back from the television station." She crossed her fingers under the surface of the water.

"I guess that means you won't be on the news tonight. Because Duane is sure to call in and tell them where to find you if he sees your face on it tonight."

Jessica turned to stare at him, forgetting to pretend disinterest.

"Uh-uh. Just as I thought. You didn't call your dad last night, did you?" His hands were on his hips, which only emphasized his broad chest and trim hips.

Jessica turned back to the dishes.

"Jessica?" His voice was stern, demanding.

"No, I didn't."

"Then Duane is going to be one very rich young man in the morning."

Jessica kept her gaze down, automatically washing the dishes as she tried to think what to do.

"If you called your father now, he might pull the offer before the ten o'clock news. Duane isn't going to get home in time to watch an earlier edition."

"My father has caller ID. He'll have your number and then your location in no time." She knew how quickly money could work.

"Then call the television station. Assure them that you're okay. You can tell them you had an argument with your father. Maybe that will stop it."

"Do you think so?" Her prospects brightened a little at his words.

"Can't hurt to try."

She dried her hands on a towel. "All right. I'll call the station."

He followed her into the den. "There's a Kansas City telephone directory on the bottom shelf."

"Thanks." She looked up the number, then dialed, her fingers shaking so badly she wasn't sure she'd done so correctly.

When the receptionist answered with the call letters of the station, she asked to speak to the manager. One of her father's lessons was always go to the top.

"My name is Jessica Barnes. My father ran an ad on your station last night offering a reward for my location."

"Yes, Miss Barnes. How may I help you?"

"Could you tell my father I'm safe and will be home Saturday or Sunday?"

"I'll be glad to pass on the message, but if you pardon me for asking, why can't you call him?"

"We've had an argument, and I'm not ready to talk to him yet."

"Don't you think—"

"I'd prefer that the ad not run this evening."

"I'll pass the message on to your father, but that decision has to be his."

"Thank you," she said before she hung up.

"Well?" Rob stood leaning against the door, his arms crossed over his chest.

"He said he'd let him know I called, but whether the ad runs is up to my father." She began pacing back and forth across the room. "When will you be able to drive on the roads?"

"I'm not sure. If the snow stops tonight, we might be able to get out tomorrow."

"If you can, would you take me to the nearest town?"

"Yeah, but I'm not sure they can pull out your car and repair it all in one day."

"I can rent a car."

"You seem awfully determined to get the hell out of Dodge."

She whirled around to glare at him. "This isn't a joke. I don't want my father to know where I am."

"That much is obvious. But I think it's about time for you to explain why."

"No. It's my business. I appreciate your letting

me stay here, but I don't think it's necessary to confide all my secrets to you."

They stared at each other across the room. Jessica didn't think she could hold his gaze much longer, when he started walking toward her.

"Then maybe I'll beat Duane at collecting that reward money."

Chapter Seven

Jessica gasped and took a step back when Rob reached out for her. Her cheeks turned so pale he thought she was going to faint.

"Are you all right?" he asked, but he withdrew his hands.

"Yes," she replied, her voice frigid. "How much?"

Rob looked at her, puzzled. "How much what?"

"How much money do you want?"

He stared at her, missing the smile that could light up her face, the interest in her blue eyes, the warmth that had him tingling all over. In the place of that appealing woman was a block of ice.

"From you?" he asked.

"Yes, from me. How much money will it take to keep you from telling my dad where I am?"

"How much are you offering?" He'd guessed she came from a wealthy background. Now he'd find out how wealthy.

"Five thousand."

"That's all?"

Her chin rose. "Ten."

"Paltry."

"Fifty, and that's as high as I can go."

"It must be real important for you to avoid your father. What's the problem?"

"You think I'd tell you? You're ready to sell me out. Dad always said money talks. But I don't."

"Sweetheart, I don't want your money. I was trying to see how important it is that you avoid your father. You're the one who said you could handle everything, that you weren't in trouble. If that's true, why are you running?"

"Sweetheart? You think a few honeyed words will smooth over your greediness? I'm not a fool. I've seen how people react to money." She tried to push past him, for the door.

Taking her arms, he held her firmly but gently. "Jess, talk to me. What's going on?"

The ice began cracking, but she wouldn't confide in him. The tears that pooled in her big blue eyes spilled over, one at a time, but she kept her chin up. "I can't trust you. Besides, you're worse off than me. You're going to go to jail. And I don't know what will happen to Cathy and Michael."

"Don't be ridiculous. Tell me what I can do to help you."

"You can't—"

The phone rang and she jumped as if she'd been pinched.

He leaned over and picked up the phone, keeping one hand on her arm. "Hello?"

"Is this 555-6703?" a gruff voice demanded.

"Yes."

"I want to speak to Jessica Barnes."

"Jessica Barnes?" he repeated, raising one eyebrow at his companion. The panic on her face worried him. "I think you must have a wrong number. No one by that name lives here."

"I know she doesn't live there. But she's there. Put her on the phone."

"Did you know we're in the middle of a snowstorm out here? My children and I arrived Wednesday afternoon and no one has come here since, except for a couple of skiers. We've been snowed in."

"There must be some mistake. My daughter called the television station from this number today. You're lying."

Rob already knew he didn't like anyone who upset Jessica as much as her father had, even though he didn't know the particulars. Now he knew he didn't like the man for his own reasons, too. "I don't appreciate being called a liar." After all, he might have skirted the truth, but he hadn't outright lied. Jessica arrived before him and his kids.

"I'm offering a reward for word of her."

"Really? How much?"

Jessica tried to wrest her arm from his hold when she heard his question, but he held her by his side.

"Ten thousand dollars."

"Too bad I can't help you. I could use that money."

"I might double it if I received information at once."

"Well, hell, if I find her in one of the snowdrifts,

I'll give you a call. You will pay dead or alive, won't you?"

Jessica stiffened, her eyes growing large, and he almost laughed out loud.

"This is not a joking matter!" his caller snapped.

"I apologize, but since she did telephone someone you can assume she's safe. So if I were you, I'd save my money. After all, that's all you're concerned about—her safety, isn't it?"

There was a telling silence before the man hurriedly assured him of his accuracy. "But I need to talk to her. Just to be sure she's all right."

"You know," Rob said, as if considering the past events, "it's strange that she'd call a television station instead of you. Did you do something to hurt her?"

"Of course not! She's my daughter. Are you sure she's not there?"

"I'm sure."

"Write down my number in case you run across her."

Rob pretended an interest in the number the man gave, even going so far as to ask him to repeat the last four numbers, as if he were writing it down.

He could feel Jessica's gaze on him, watching his every move. Did she finally realize he was on her side? He hoped so.

Hanging up the phone, he looked at her. "Guess who?"

"My father."

"Well, I'm assuming that was the identity of the gentleman. He never actually gave his name." He smiled at her and felt the slightest bit of relaxation in her arm.

"You didn't tell him I'm here."

"Nope."

"You didn't write down the number."

"Nope."

"Do you have a photographic memory?"

"Nope. But I know how to call information. Does that count?" He cocked one eyebrow at her, hoping to see her smile again.

Instead she sighed and leaned her head against his chest. "Thank you."

He encircled her with both arms, enjoying the feel of her pressed against him. Her face nestled against his neck and he stroked her hair, loving the silkiness of it. Unfortunately he couldn't let her believe she'd escaped her father.

"You know he'll be here first thing tomorrow."

"But you told him I wasn't here." Her arms went around his neck and she pressed closer against him.

"Sweetheart, I don't for a minute think he believed me. And this phone number is the only lead he has."

"Oh." She paused, still leaning against him. Then, to his surprise, she reached up and kissed his cheek. "Thanks for trying, anyway."

He couldn't answer because his body reacted to her lips touching him. His mouth craved equal time, and he covered her lips with his. Their earlier kisses were nothing compared to this celebration of the tension that had flowed between them.

He demanded she open to him, eager to deepen

their embrace…and their relationship. It didn't matter that his children were upstairs, that she was in trouble, that he intended to concentrate on being a dad. It only mattered that she was in his arms, and he never wanted to let her go.

She pulled away from him, her lips escaping his. He wanted her with every ounce of him. As he pursued her lips, however, she turned away. "No!"

"Jess," he pleaded, his lips tracing her jawline, the nearest silky skin he could reach. "Baby, come on, let me…help you."

She pushed out of his embrace, but he noted her fingers were shaking. She felt as he did; he knew it.

When she resisted his seeking hands, turning even more away from him, he tried to bring himself under control. He could be patient. Of course he could.

"Tell me what's wrong between you and your father." He had to get her to open up to him. All along, she'd held back. Until that kiss.

She had moved away and crossed her arms over her chest, as if she were cold. "You wouldn't understand."

"Jess, don't you realize yet that I'm on your side? Whatever he did, I know you wouldn't have run away unless you had a good reason. I'll help you."

She remained silent for so long he thought she wasn't going to respond. With hunger surging through him, the desire to hold her against him again, to make her his, he moved closer.

She must have sensed his approach because she turned and held out a hand. He almost chuckled that she would think that delicate limb would stop him.

He'd start his kisses with each finger and work his way up her arm.

But he was wrong. She stopped him cold.

"My marriage. It's my marriage."

He turned to stone, dismay filling him. She was married? The woman who'd broken into his life, who'd undermined his promise to learn to be a good father, who'd seduced him with her sweetness, was married?

JESSICA REALIZED Rob had the wrong impression. He'd been so sweet and supportive until she'd spoken. Then anger and dismay had filled his eyes. She wanted to reassure him, but before she could, they were interrupted.

"Daddy?" Cathy called just before she stepped into the room.

"What is it, Cathy?" Rob demanded harshly, his gaze never leaving Jessica. She tried a tentative smile, but that made him look away. He acted as if he hated her.

"We're bored. What can we do now?"

Rob stared at his child as if she were a martian.

Jessica decided she should help him. After all, he'd tried to help her even if he had misunderstood. And maybe she could work in an explanation that would erase the anger in his eyes.

"Do you have any puzzles here?" she asked. "I used to do puzzles when the weather was bad. We could all work on one together at the kitchen table."

"Do we, Daddy?"

"Maybe," he growled, showing no appreciation

for Jessica's suggestion. "Go look in the closet at the end of the hall upstairs and see what you can find."

As soon as Cathy left, Jessica seized her opportunity. "Rob, I didn't—"

He turned his back to her. "Don't you think you should've mentioned your marriage before we—before I—"

His accusation irritated her. "I didn't ask you to kiss me like that."

"You sure as hell didn't protest! I should've known. You're just like other women. No morals! Out for what you can get!"

All Jessica's appreciation for Rob's actions disappeared in an instant. "How dare you! I have done nothing wrong! I will not be accused like that!"

"No, of course not! That's another womanly trait, isn't it? Blaming whatever goes wrong in a relationship on someone else. Saying I should be around to entertain you!"

Jessica recognized at once that Rob was talking from personal experience. But it had nothing to do with her. "Listen, Rob, whatever your problems, they're not my fault."

"Oh, yeah? Do you think I would've kissed Mother Goose like I just kissed you? She wouldn't tempt me like you do. Or lead me on, letting me kiss her, without telling me she's married!"

He was charging around the cleared space as if he were demented, or being attacked by fire ants. But his words had reminded Jessica why he was upset.

"I'm not married."

He froze, then slowly turned to face her. "What did you say?"

She swallowed, concerned by the threatening stare he cast on her. "I—I said I'm not married."

"But you just said you were."

"No, I didn't. You asked what was the problem between me and my father and I said... Well, I meant to say... Look, I'm not married. But my father wants me to be."

"We found one!" Cathy announced, bursting through the door, a cardboard box lifted over her head.

"I helped pick it out," Michael assured them as the two children entered the room.

SO MUCH FOR ROB'S PROMISE to himself to put his children first. He wanted his children to go away, back upstairs. To watch television, or nap, or whatever children did by themselves. The desperate need to discover the meaning of Jessica's words was almost overwhelming.

"Great," Jessica responded, though without much enthusiasm, but her words seemed to satisfy the children. Cathy took her hand and led the way to the table.

"I'll fix us drinks," Rob said as the kids and Jessica began sorting out the puzzle. "Uh, Jessica, could you help me?"

"I'll help, Daddy," Cathy offered. Before she could get out of her chair, Rob stopped her. "No, sweetheart. You work on the puzzle. Jessica will help me.''

Though she looked wary of him, telling Rob his demeanor might be too fierce, Jessica came to the counter.

"Explain!" he ordered in a whisper.

"I told you," she whispered in return. Then with a sigh, she added, "I was engaged but I decided to break it off. My father and Stephen refused to accept my decision."

"Stephen?" Unreasonable jealousy filled him. He didn't even know the man.

"Jessica, look! I found a cow eye!" Michael called out, holding up a piece of the puzzle.

"Terrific, Michael," she replied with a smile.

Rob wanted her attention turned toward him again. "What do you mean?"

"I tried to cancel the engagement party we'd scheduled, but my father reinstated the orders. I told Stephen I wouldn't marry him, and he assured me I would."

"So what did you do?"

"Daddy, how come you and Jessica are whispering?" Cathy asked, looking up from the puzzle.

"Uh, we're trying to decide who gets what glass."

"Okay, I want the Indian Princess one," Cathy told him and returned to the puzzle.

"I ran away. I know that sounds childish," she hurriedly said, "but I thought Dad would cancel the party, or at least not announce the engagement. It seemed the simplest way to handle everything."

"Do you love him? Stephen, I mean." He hadn't intended to ask that question, but he needed to know the answer.

"No."

There was no hesitation in her answer. Rob breathed a little easier.

"I thought I did at first. He can be charming. But then I found some old love letters from my mother to my father. I'd already had doubts, but after reading those letters, I knew what I felt wasn't love."

He wanted to ask her what she felt now, this very moment, about him, about them, but he didn't. For one thing, he hadn't worked out his own feelings. Except for wanting her. After all, in spite of his desire for her, he had to think of his kids.

"What are you going to do now?"

She sighed. "I don't know. If Dad gets here in the morning before I can get away, I'll have to fight him. I wanted to avoid that. But I'm not going to be sold into marriage."

"You think that's what he's trying to do?"

Reluctantly, her face troubled, she nodded. "I think he and Stephen have some financial dealings. I didn't make the connection at first, but we started going out about the time Dad got a loan from Stephen."

Rob frowned. He supposed such arrangements still happened, but he hated to think of Jessica being used in such a way. The urge to slap on his white hat and play the hero filled him.

When he stared over her shoulder out the window, contemplating his choices, he discovered something important. "It's stopped snowing. In fact, the snow seems to be melting. The temperature must've risen. Cathy, go upstairs and turn on the television. See if you can find some kind of weather report."

ROB'S OBSERVATIONS didn't cheer Jessica any. They only confirmed what she'd earlier suspected. Her father would be there in the morning. When Rob, followed by Michael, left the kitchen after Cathy called him, she remained where she was, staring out the window.

The three Berensons came back into the kitchen.

Rob spoke first. "Go pack whatever you brought with you, Jessica."

"Why?" Was he throwing her out? Was he disgusted by her story?

"Because we're going to drive back to Kansas City tonight."

"What? Why?" She watched him closely. Maybe he'd decided to accept her father's offer. Her shoulders slumped.

"The three of us have talked it over, and we're ready to go back to Kansas City. You need to get out of here before your father shows up. And we want to help you."

She looked at three faces, each one dear to her now, and gave them a wobbly smile, relief filling her. At least Rob wasn't selling her out to her father. "I guess I can find somewhere to hide in Kansas City for a day or two. Thank you. I appreciate your cutting short your holiday for me."

"No problem. And we have a place for you to hide."

She stared at Rob, unsure what he meant.

"You can stay with us!" Cathy exclaimed, grabbing her hand and jumping up and down.

She was touched, but she knew their idea wouldn't work. After all, her father already had Rob's phone number. He'd soon have a name to go with the number. "Thanks, sweetheart, but I'm afraid my father would soon find me there. He'll know your daddy's name."

"That's the beauty of our plan," Rob told her, grinning. "I haven't bought a house yet. We're staying in my ex-wife's house until I can find what I want. It's not in my name."

Hope began burgeoning in Jessica. "Really? Are you sure you don't mind? Can we get through? I don't want to endanger the children."

"I wouldn't consider it if I thought for a minute they could be hurt. The plows have hit the road and the snow is melting."

"Oh, Rob," Jessica said with a sigh and a beaming smile. "Thank you so much."

"Don't thank me yet. We've got some work to do to get packed and out of here. You kids grab something to eat. Jess and I will be upstairs stripping the beds and packing, okay?"

"Okay, Daddy," Cathy cheerfully agreed.

Michael, of course, wasn't going to argue about food.

Once she and Rob were out of the kitchen, she stopped him as he headed for the stairs. "Rob, thank you again,'' she said and threw her arms around his neck.

His lips didn't hesitate to take hers in a thorough kiss, but much to her disappointment, he ended it quickly. "I like the way you say thank-you, but let's postpone it until we're out of here. Your father may move faster than we think."

She nodded in agreement, glad he was no longer angry, and he took her hand to pull her upstairs behind him.

A few minutes later, they met at the top of the stairway, both with their arms full. Jessica knew she and Rob had a few things to work out, at least she hoped they did, but the first thing she needed to do was escape her father's clutches.

The tension on Rob's face reminded her again of the trouble she was causing him and his children. "Thanks again, Rob."

"Don't thank me now. We're not out of the woods yet, Goldilocks," he teased, a brief smile on his lips.

"*Ugh,* what a bad pun!"

"Yeah. Come on. We don't have any time to spare." Without waiting for a reply, he started down the stairs.

Then he came to an abrupt halt.

Someone was pounding on the front door.

Chapter Eight

Jessica grasped Rob's arm with shaky fingers. "Rob," she whispered.

"Go into the kitchen. Stay there and keep the kids quiet," he said, his voice barely audible.

She nodded and tiptoed the rest of the way down the stairs. He followed her, stowing the suitcases in the den before approaching the front door. He hadn't thought her father could get here that fast.

Swinging open the door, he stared at the short man in work clothes. Funny, he hadn't pictured Jessica's father like this. "Yes?"

"I thought someone was here," the man replied with a big grin. "Listen, I know the snow's melting, but we're clearing off the road, and when I saw your lights, I thought you might want the snow plowed off the driveway, too. No charge. The city's paying. Okay?"

Rob hid his sigh of relief. "That would be great. Thanks for asking."

"Didn't know anyone was living out here this time of the year."

"We're not. We just came for Thanksgiving and got caught by the snow." And Goldilocks.

"Well, Mother Nature's taking care of your problems, now. By tomorrow afternoon, everything should be clear. Now I can remember back in..."

Rob didn't think the man would ever stop reminiscing. All the while, Jessica was hiding in the kitchen having heart failure, thinking it was her father.

"Thanks for the offer," Rob broke in. "My family's waiting dinner on me."

"Oh, no problem. Go enjoy."

He closed the door as the man headed toward a snowplow smack-dab in the middle of the lane that led to the house. With the lane and the driveway cleared, he knew they could make it to Kansas City tonight.

When he reached the kitchen, Jessica and his children were in a tight huddle against the door that led to the garage.

"All clear. It was the snowplow driver, offering to clear our driveway."

He watched with appreciation as a big sigh ran through Jessica's body. And wished he could hold her in his arms. But his children were watching the two of them, and now wasn't the time.

"Did you two finish your dinner?" Rob asked his children with a brisk tone.

"Yes, Daddy," Cathy assured him. Michael didn't look as convinced.

"What is it, Michael?"

"I didn't get any coconut cake."

"We'll take it with us and you can have it tomorrow."

"What about tonight?" the boy persisted.

"I'll buy you a candy bar. That reminds me, Cathy, would you go get the pillows and the blankets from your two beds? You may want to go to sleep before we get to Kansas City."

"Will it take that long?" Jessica asked.

"With the snow we'll have to go slowly. I doubt that we'll get to Kansas City before midnight."

"Will Mrs. Hutchins be expecting us?"

"She will after I call her. But I don't want to call from here. Your father might get hold of the phone records and it would lead him straight to the house."

"Yes, you're right. That's something he would do." She sent him an apologetic look.

Rob grinned. "Don't worry about it. I've dealt with worse."

Cathy, trailed by Michael, returned to the kitchen. "Daddy, why are our suitcases in the den? Aren't we going to take them with us?"

"Yes, we are. Thanks for reminding me." He turned to Jessica. "How's the kitchen going? Have you thrown everything out? If you have, I'll take out the trash as soon as I get the bags."

"No, I was too—I didn't do anything earlier. I was afraid we'd make too much noise. I'll start now."

Within half an hour, they were all loaded in Rob's four-wheel-drive vehicle and backing out of the now cleared driveway.

Jessica looked back with longing. The little house in the woods had been a wonderful sanctuary.

"You can come back to visit anytime," Rob said softly, looking at her.

"Thanks. I may take you up on that offer."

"All set, kids?" he called to his children in the rear seat. With pillows, blankets and a favorite toy, they seemed content.

He put the car in Drive, and they were on their way.

Jessica breathed a sigh of relief.

"Don't count your chickens too soon, Goldilocks," he warned. "We need to get off this road, and preferably through a town or two, before we're safe. We don't want your father seeing what kind of vehicle we're driving."

"But you said he probably wouldn't come until in the morning."

"And I hope I'm right. But I can't be sure, now that the snow stopped."

She nodded. "I was so frightened earlier. It's not that I won't face my father, and Stephen, too. I already have once. But they ignored me and went ahead with the plans, as if they could coerce me. I guess that spooked me."

"Can't say I blame you."

"I promise I won't stay long. Just until Saturday morning."

"We won't be in any hurry for you to leave. My ex's house is huge."

"It's nice of her to let you live there until you find a place of your own."

"She'd prefer that we stay there until they come back. The company promised them they'd only have to stay in South America for five years."

"Then why don't you?"

"Because I want my own place. I don't want to worry if I want to put my feet on the coffee table." He looked at her, grinning. "I'm not a high society type."

"But if the children live there, it can't be too prim and proper, can it?"

"That's one of the reasons I want my own place. The kids are pretty much relegated to their rooms."

Jessica looked over her shoulder. "Well, your ex can't be all bad, Rob, or you wouldn't have such wonderful children."

"That's true. But we want our own place," he repeated stubbornly.

"So the Hutchinses won't be around to help out forever?"

"Oh, yeah. They're coming with us."

"Really?"

"Yeah. They only stayed after the divorce to look after the kids. They've worked for my family for a long time."

A shiver ran down Jessica's spine. "Don't tell me Mr. Hutchins is retired from your line of work?"

"My line of work? What are you talking about?"

She looked over her shoulder again, to be sure the children weren't paying attention. "You know," she whispered, "like Sims."

He grinned. "No, Hutchins never worked for anyone like Sims."

"Oh, good."

They were approaching the county road, where Jessica had had her problem with her car. Rob slowed down at the intersection.

"Maybe you'd better duck down until we're out on the highway. If someone comes along and sees you in the front seat, they might—"

"Right." Jessica didn't need things spelled out. She was more eager to avoid her father than Rob. Scooting down, she kept her head below the window level.

"What are you doing, Jessica?" Cathy asked, leaning forward as much as her seat belt would allow.

"Uh, I'm playing a game. Your father is going to, um, pick out something he can see, and then I have to guess what it is. It's called I Spy."

"I want to play! I want to play!" screamed Cathy, bouncing in her seat.

"Then hide your eyes, like Jessica," Rob quickly said.

"Me, too." Michael wrapped his chubby little arm over his eyes.

"Okay, I'm looking for something. Everyone stay down."

Jessica felt the truck come to a halt and then turn left. "Are you looking?" she whispered.

"Yeah." After a pause, he added, "Your car's still there. I don't see anything…yet. Stay down."

"Daddy? Is it time yet?" Cathy called.

"Not yet, sweetheart."

The truck picked up speed, though Rob still

wasn't driving fast. She'd be glad when they were far away from the little road to Rob's house. Suddenly she noticed light increasing in the front of the vehicle.

Night had fallen before they left the house, so she knew the extra light had to be coming from a vehicle on the road. "Who is it?" she whispered, tensing.

"I'd say it's your father since we're talking long, black limo."

She gasped. "He only called a couple of hours ago."

"I would imagine he flew into the county airport and hired that limo. There's only one around here that I know of."

"Does the limo company know you?"

"Not really. And they won't recognize this vehicle because I just bought it last week in Kansas City."

"Daddy, isn't it time yet?" Cathy called, interrupting their whispering.

Jessica watched as Rob studied his rearview mirror. "As soon as I get over the next hill, sweetheart, I'll find something. Be patient."

"Are they turning?" Jessica whispered.

"Yeah. Our timing was perfect."

Perfect? Another five minutes and she would've been caught. She didn't like to cut things that close. "Can I get up now?"

"Yeah. Okay, Cathy, Michael, I found something."

"How do we guess?" Cathy asked.

"You have to ask your daddy questions, and he

can only answer with yes or no,'' Jessica instructed, trying to keep her voice steady.

By the time Rob stopped the car to phone Mrs. Hutchins, they were all tired of the game. Jessica quickly took Cathy to the bathroom and then got back into the car, keeping a low profile. She assumed her father would fly back to Kansas City, but she didn't want to take any chances of seeing him, now that she'd gotten away.

When Rob and Michael came back to the car, they each carried two colas.

Rob placed them all on the hood until he was sure they were belted securely. Then he gave each child a drink and a candy bar, which he fished out of his pocket.

He turned to Jessica. ''Got your seat belt fastened?''

''Yes. Does that mean I get a candy bar, too?'' she asked with a grin.

''Yes, ma'am.'' With a flourish he pulled out two more candy bars and gave her one.

Contented silence had already fallen over the back seat. For the next hour as they drove, they quietly listened to easy music on the radio. Even though Jessica should be preparing how she would face her father, she found herself drifting off to the romantic music, her gaze turning frequently to the big man beside her. She wondered if she'd ever see him again, once she'd settled her problems with her father. She hoped so. There was some elemental connection between the two of them that she'd never felt before.

And she meant more than the physical. Though there was no question that when he touched her, she reacted differently than she'd ever done before. But she trusted him. She felt safe as well as excited when she was with him.

With Stephen, she'd wondered a number of times if he even knew anything about her feelings. Or cared. Rob, on the other hand, seemed to read her mind. Sometimes when she didn't want him to.

Only when she'd said she was married, or at least that was how Rob had interpreted it, had she felt shut out. But they'd straightened out that misunderstanding, and she'd found the warmth in his eyes again.

"Maybe you can ease the cover over Michael?" Rob whispered.

She turned around to see both children were asleep. Cathy was snuggled under a blanket, but Michael had kicked his into the floorboard. Reaching down, she pulled the blanket back over the little boy.

"There, he's all tucked in." She relaxed back into her seat.

"Good, because we need to talk."

Something in his voice warned her the conversation wasn't going to be pleasant. Had he changed his mind about letting her stay at his house? She tried to think of what had gone wrong, but nothing came to mind. "Okay."

"Have you thought about what you're going to tell your father?"

"No. Not really. Just that I don't intend to marry Stephen, no matter how much he likes him."

"Is that what he told you? That he wants you to marry him because *he* likes Stephen?"

"Yes. You don't understand. It's more than I said. My father always wanted a son. I...I tried to do...to be the son he wanted, but it's impossible." She shrugged her shoulders, hoping to hide the deep hurt she'd felt most of her life.

"And I'm grateful," Rob said, reaching over to take her hand in his and squeeze it gently.

And that's why she lov—really liked Rob. He was sensitive to her difficulties. "Thanks."

"Do you think that'll be enough to discourage him?"

"No. But this is the nineties. It's not like they can force me."

"Your father can cut off your funds."

Was he worried that she couldn't pay him for his help? She hated to be so suspicious of him, but she'd had experiences with men after her money. "I have some money, so if you're worried about me paying you back—"

"For what?"

"Well, I did offer to pay room and board."

"And I turned you down. Everything doesn't always have to come down to money, Jessica." He didn't sound mad, but his voice was cooler.

She bit her bottom lip, trying to figure out what the man wanted. Finally she said, "I have a trust fund from my mother."

"And you realize you may lose your job?"

"Lose my job? Why would I—you mean my father would fire me for not doing what he said? Surely you don't think—''

''I'm afraid I do, sweetheart.''

''But I'm a damned good accountant.'' She sat up straight and squared her shoulders. ''I'll find another job.''

''I'm just worried about this financial angle you mentioned. What does this Stephen of yours do for a living?''

''He's not *my* Stephen,'' Jessica protested. Then she considered Rob's question. ''He runs an investment fund, but he doesn't talk much about it.''

''In Kansas City?''

''Yes. But he only moved to Kansas City about nine months ago. Dad met him, oh, I guess, three months later.''

''Where'd he come from?''

''Chicago.''

Something about Rob's demeanor alerted her. ''What's wrong with Chicago?''

''Nothing. What's Stephen's last name?''

''Cattaloni.''

''Damn! That's all I need.''

''What are you talking about?''

He took his hand away, and she felt cold all over. When he didn't respond, staring straight ahead of him into the dark night, she prodded him. ''Rob? What's wrong?''

He heaved a sigh, as if the weight of the world were on his back. ''I may be wrong.''

''About what?''

"Did you know that Stephen Cattaloni has mob connections?"

She was grateful for the darkness so that Rob couldn't see how shocked she was. Mob connections? How would Rob know—the realization that came to her was even more shocking. It would be upsetting to think that she'd almost married someone of that ilk. But she figured the only way Rob would know about Stephen was if he, too, associated with the wrong group of people.

"Rob, no!"

"I'm sorry, sweetheart."

"Please don't tell me—"

"Jessica, listen to me. I know what I'm talking about."

That's what I'm afraid of. She covered her ears with her hands. "I don't want to hear this."

Because she couldn't believe she'd made the same mistake twice. First she got engaged to a mobster. Then she fell—almost fell in love with another one? Was there something wrong with her, that she'd follow such a pattern? What did the pop psychologists call it?

She knew her hands wouldn't keep her from hearing whatever he said, but he apparently accepted her protest. He said nothing, merely continued to drive.

Finally, feeling foolish, she took her hands down. He slid his gaze her way, then back to the road, and said nothing.

Okay. He was going to abide by her wishes and say nothing else. For a little while longer, she could pretend that he was a nice guy, a terrific father and the best kisser she'd ever met. And nothing else. No mob. No bad guy. No mayhem.

She pretended as hard as she could.

Only it wasn't enough.

Hoping to give him another chance to deny what he'd just confessed, she demanded, outrage in her voice, "How can you look at yourself in the mirror in the morning?"

"Look, I didn't want to tell you, but you have to know what you're dealing with." His voice was hoarse, as if under a strain.

"I know, but—" She broke off, working hard to hold back the tears that were backing up in her throat. She'd thought him tender, protective. How could she have made such a mistake? She gasped. His children. Had he given no thought to his children? "Have you—have you made provisions for the children? I mean, will—"

"What are you talking about? What does Stephen Cattaloni have to do with my children?"

"Oh, please, Rob, I'm not an idiot!"

"Well, I must be because I don't know what you're talking about!"

His jaw was clenched and she had the biggest urge to reach over and massage it, relax it, kiss it. She tightened her fingers into a fist. She was beating a dead horse. The man wasn't what she thought he was if he could mix with criminals and not be concerned about what would happen with his kids.

"Never mind."

"We can't just end the conversation here, Jess," Rob said, almost pleading.

"Why not? You've said what you have to say. I know about Stephen now, though I find it hard to believe. He's accepted everywhere."

"That's one of his best traits, as far as the mob goes," Rob said dryly.

"Is that—" She stopped. She wanted to ask if his own good manners and incredible looks is what had made him valuable to the criminal element, but she couldn't say those words. Because he was a lot better at duping naive women than Stephen was. He'd taken her in completely.

"What?"

"Nothing."

"Look, Jessica, this is hard to say, but think about the setup here."

"What setup?"

"Your dad and Stephen."

"What are you talking about?"

"You said the business wasn't doing so well a few months ago. Your dad was upset. Then everything straightened out with a loan from Stephen."

"So? Every business goes through bad patches."

"What turned everything around?"

Fear was seeping into her already unhappy head. What was he suggesting? "I don't know. Dad said sales picked up, that's all."

"Sales? Or Stephen's money?"

He didn't say anything else, but he didn't have to. He'd given her plenty to think about. If her father was receiving a steady supply of funds from Stephen to keep the company afloat, it would explain her father's attitude toward her marriage. And who knew what Stephen intended to ask for those loans? Was he laundering the mob's money through Barnes Enterprises?

"You can't know that they're doing anything wrong," she protested harshly.

"No, I can't. But I suspect that's what's happening. And what if good old Stephen took a liking to you and made you part of the bargain? That would explain why your dad refused to let you back out of the engagement. Why he's so eager to find you before tomorrow night."

He didn't look at her, and she was glad. She felt sick to her stomach. Staunchly she shrugged back her shoulders. "I won't believe it until I see proof."

"You won't see proof unless you look for it."

Her eyes burned but she stared straight ahead, her chin up. "If you're implying that I would cooperate in something illegal, you're wrong. *Some* of us have morals."

"And your father?"

That sucker punch took her breath away. "I—I don't know. I just hope I discover the truth—and find a way to protect him before the police find out."

"Uh, Jess, there's something I've neglected to tell you."

"You mean there's more bad news?" She wasn't sure she could handle any more. After all, what could be worse than her father, her ex-fiancé and Rob were all—all bad guys, she finally admitted with a sob.

"Well, uh, you see...I'm FBI."

Chapter Nine

"Yes, of course, that's been obvious all along," she said with a laugh.

Rob tried to see her face in the dark, but until a car passed them from the opposite direction, he couldn't. When the headlights hit them, however, he read her look of disbelief. "You think I'm lying?"

"If you were with the FBI, you would've told me long before now, Rob."

"We're trained not to tell, Jess. I was undercover for a long time. Besides, women react strangely." His wife had. Some women were attracted to the danger and excitement—until they realized that same danger and excitement meant unreliability. Not being there at the drop of a hat.

"Undercover? Let me guess. With the mob?"

"Yes," he agreed, relieved that finally she understood.

"Oh, Rob," she said softly, almost mournfully. "Don't."

"Don't what?"

"Don't lie to try to convince me you're a good guy."

When her words hit him, he whipped his head around to stare at her. What the hell was she talking about?

"Watch out. You're driving," she warned.

He turned his gaze back to the road, but his mind was trying to understand what had just happened. "You don't believe me?"

"It's all right, Rob. I figured things out the first time I overheard you on the phone. I don't approve, and I'm worried about the children. But what's done is done."

He risked another glance at her. She looked like the all-American girl, her blond hair touching her shoulders, her blue eyes bright. Only her lips showed any sign of stress, trembling when she tried to smile. He wished he could pull over and comfort them, as he had in the cabin.

Just thinking about kissing her brought about a reaction that he didn't want just then. Hell! How could he want to kiss her when she believed he was a criminal?

"What is it you're saying I'm guilty of?"

"I don't know. But you promised to cause mayhem. Mayhem is bad. I know that much."

"For the bad guys. Mayhem for the bad guys, Jess."

Instead of answering, she sniffed. His head swiveled toward her again. She couldn't be crying. But there was another sniff. Yes, a definite sniff.

He braked and pulled off the road. "Sweetheart, are you crying?"

"No," she assured him, but tears were in her voice.

He put the vehicle into Park, punched on the emergency lights and released his seat belt.

"No, Rob, don't—" Jessica began, but he ignored her words and reached for her.

"Why are you crying?"

"Because I don't want you to be—be a bad guy."

What a ridiculous situation. He'd never had to prove his innocence before. "Jess, I swear, I work for the FBI. I'm a good guy."

She snuggled against him, sniffing again. "If that's true, show me your badge."

Damn. Damn. Damn.

"Uh, Jess, I wasn't quite accurate when I said I'm with the FBI."

She grew very still in his arms. "What do you mean?"

"Well, I *was* with the FBI. I resigned to take care of my children. Last week."

She said nothing but she pushed against his chest, trying to put distance between them.

"It's true. Until last week I worked for the FBI. But when I quit, I turned in my badge and ID, of course, so I can't— Can't you just take my word?"

"Yes, of course," she said, but her words were as stiff as her body, pushing away from him.

"Jessica, surely you can take my word? I thought you trusted me. I'm trying to help you."

"That doesn't mean—that's why it's so hard. Just because you can be nice doesn't mean—I understand, Rob."

"What do you understand?"

"Maybe you got started down the wrong road before you realized how bad it— Never mind."

"I don't believe this. You're condemning me with no proof."

"You're not offering any proof. Should I believe you're a good guy because you're a great kisser?" she asked, frustration filling her voice.

He paused in his defense. "You think I'm a great kisser?"

She rolled her eyes and looked away. "Just start driving again."

"I think I'd rather—"

"Daddy," a sleepy voice intruded. "Are we home yet?"

Rob gave up and slid back behind the wheel. Jessica wasn't going to believe him. Not right now. He'd worry about persuading her tomorrow. When they were alone. "We'll be home soon, little one."

He pulled the truck back onto the road, fastening his seat belt as he did. He was ready for this ridiculous trip to be over.

JESSICA REMAINED crunched in her corner of the four-wheel-drive, watching the road as it slid beneath the wheels. What a strange two days she'd experienced. Her panic at the trap her father seemed to be springing on her that led her to flee. The slide into a ditch in the snowstorm, followed by her trek through the woods to Rob's house.

Two days spent with Rob and his children.

How could two days change her life so completely?

Especially when one of the three bears wasn't exactly lily white. With a hysterical giggle quickly stifled, she reminded herself that if he were lily white, Rob Berenson would be a polar bear. A quick look at the virile man next to her reminded her that there was nothing cold about him.

Nope. He was hot stuff.

Another giggle floated up her throat, but she kept it from escaping. Probably hot with the police, too. Suddenly she felt more like crying than laughing. How could she run from one inappropriate man and fall for one just as bad? Did she have a masochistic personality?

"We're here," Rob said softly as he slowed and turned into a circular driveway in front of a large house.

Jessica let out a long sigh. She wasn't looking forward to staying in Rob's ex-wife's house, but it would provide a haven from her father. And she'd still be close to Rob, even if that wasn't in her best interest.

After the car stopped, she released her seat belt and turned to free the sleeping children. "I'll carry Michael," she said, choosing the smaller of the two.

"Okay, thanks." Rob went to ring the doorbell, then, without waiting for an answer, he came back to get Cathy.

In spite of the rising temperature there was still a chill in the air. Michael's warm body, wrapped in his blanket, provided some welcome warmth as Jessica moved around the vehicle. When the door came into view, she discovered an elderly couple waiting on the front step.

"Come right this way, Jessica," the lady said, surprising her. "You must be exhausted, poor dear. It's so good of you to help Robbie with the children."

"Thank you. I hope I'm not imposing too much—"

"Don't be silly," Mrs. Hutchins said with motherly tones, guiding her into the house. "Just follow me and we'll have that little fellow in his own bed at once."

Jessica did as she'd been told and followed Mrs. Hutchins up the broad, sweeping staircase. As she went, she studied the house, remembering Rob's words.

Everything was gilt and antique, a showplace for Junior League or whatever society club their mother belonged to. But it didn't have the appearance of a home.

Once she'd laid Michael on his bed and assisted Mrs. Hutchins in undressing him in a room that was perfect for a little boy, the older woman led her out into the hall.

"I prepared the room next to Robbie's for you. It has its own bath. He said you didn't have any luggage because of the storm, so I've put a nightgown on the bed for you."

"Thank you, Mrs. Hutchins. I appreciate your hospitality."

"Never you mind, my dear. Any friend of Robbie's is a friend of ours. Do you need anything to eat or drink before you go to bed?''

"No, thank you."

Mrs. Hutchins headed back to the stairs and Jessica turned to the room the woman had indicated. She hoped there was no significance in its location. She didn't want Mrs. Hutchins thinking there was anything going on between her and Rob.

With her hand on the doorknob, she heard movement behind her. Spinning around, she found Rob leaving what she supposed was Cathy's room.

"Jess, do you have everything you need?"

"Yes." She flattened her back against the wall. His closeness made her nervous, not of him but of herself and the desire that was bubbling up in her.

"I'd tell you one more time that I'm a good guy, but I think maybe you're too tired to think."

She nodded, pleading with her eyes that he not bring up that nightmarish topic.

"It's been a long day, hasn't it?" he said as if he understood her feelings.

"Yes. Rob, I want to thank you for saving me from my father tonight. And offering me a place to stay."

He grinned, an endearing grin that made her heart speed up. "No problem, sweetheart." Then he swooped down and kissed her.

Before she could wrap her arms around his neck, which she wanted to do, he pulled away and whispered, "I'll see you in the morning," and ran down the stairs.

In the morning. At the rate she was going, in the morning she'd find herself in even more difficulties.

"Jessica, are you awake?" someone whispered, the voice penetrating her sleep. Jessica struggled to open her eyes, but it seemed more effort than it was worth. Just as she was sinking back into slumber, a small hand touched her cheek.

Her eyes popped open and she found Cathy standing beside the bed.

"Daddy said I should see if you want breakfast," Cathy explained. "I called from the door, but you didn't answer."

She smiled at the little girl and held her hand. "I suppose I should get up." Then she looked at her wristwatch. "My, it's nine o'clock. Have you eaten already?"

"No, we're all waiting on you. Nana made pancakes."

"I'll be right down, but tell everyone to go ahead without me. We wouldn't want cold pancakes, would we?"

Cathy giggled. "Not Michael. He thinks he's starving to death."

Once Cathy had left the room, Jessica grabbed a quick shower and dressed in her jeans and shirt again. She was getting very tired of her limited wardrobe.

When she discovered the big table in the kitchen, surrounded by Rob, his children and the Hutchinses, they all greeted her warmly.

"We thought you were Sleeping Beauty instead of Goldilocks this morning," Rob said.

"Sorry if I kept you waiting."

"Nonsense," Mrs. Hutchins replied. "You deserved to sleep, getting in at the time you did last night. It's just that these little rascals were starving."

"Michael's always starving," Cathy and Rob said simultaneously and then laughed.

Before Jessica could speak, Mrs. Hutchins placed a plate piled high with pancakes in front of her. She did a great imitation of Michael as she dug into the breakfast.

Rob, lingering over a cup of coffee, waited until she'd eaten before he asked, "What do you want to do today?"

"I'd like to go shopping."

Mr. Hutchins laughed. "Sounds like a woman," he added. His wife immediately reprimanded him, bringing a grin to Rob's face.

"You'll be able to go back home tomorrow. Sure you want to spend money on clothes?"

"Quite sure. I'm getting sick and tired of these jeans and shirt. But it needn't concern you. I'll take a taxi."

"No, I think I'd better go with you. You don't want to run into your father or—or the other man today. That would spoil all our work at getting away."

"Don't be silly, Rob. You don't want to spend your morning shopping for women's clothes," Jessica protested.

"I want to go," Cathy interjected into their argument.

"Not today, sweetheart," Rob said, but his gaze stayed on Jessica. "Another day you can shop with Jessica, if she doesn't mind, but not today."

She turned to the little girl. "After I get a few problems taken care of, I'd love to take you shopping."

"But until those problems are taken care of, I'm sticking to you like glue, even while you're shopping," Rob added.

She caught the speculative looks from the older couple and felt her cheeks heat up. What must they be thinking? "Rob, I don't need a bodyguard."

He ignored her comment. "When will you be ready to go?"

"The stores are going to be horribly crowded. It's the biggest shopping day of the year. You'll hate it."

"Ten o'clock?" he asked.

"You're not listening to me!" she protested.

"Yes, I am, but I haven't heard anything that makes me think you don't need me. Ten o'clock?"

She gave in with a sigh. The man was hard-headed. "Ten o'clock."

"Can I show you my dolls before you leave?" Cathy asked.

"Yes, of course, as soon as we help with the dishes."

"Land's sake, child, I don't need any help. You go with Cathy."

She smiled her thanks and the two of them headed

back up the stairs. Over her shoulder she noted Rob's satisfied smile. If the man thought he'd won the war, he was wrong. He'd only won one battle.

When ten o'clock came, Jessica came back down the stairs and found Rob waiting for her. "The car's out front," he said, waving for her to precede him. Expecting the four-wheel-drive they'd traveled in last night, she was surprised to discover a Mercedes waiting for them.

"Whose car is this?"

"Mine. Don't you like it?"

"But last night—"

"I know. I thought I might need something like that for the kids. But it seems like overkill for the city."

She knew there was a lot of money to be made as a criminal, but she wished he didn't flaunt it quite so readily.

When she made no move to get into the car, he asked, "What's wrong? Isn't a Mercedes what you were driving? Don't you like them?"

"Of course," she replied and moved around the car to the passenger side, followed closely by Rob. He opened the door for her and she slid into the luxury car.

After he got in, he asked, "Where shall we shop?"

"Hall's on the Plaza," she replied automatically. The Plaza was one of the most elite shopping areas in the country.

"Aren't you worried about seeing someone you know?"

"None of my friends would shop on the day after Thanksgiving. It's much too crowded."

He made no comment as he headed the car toward the Plaza. Since his ex-wife's house was in Mission Hills, an elite neighborhood on the Kansas side of the city but still near the Plaza, it didn't take long to arrive. As Jessica had predicted, the store had just opened but was already teeming with customers.

"I, um, I need to buy lingerie," she said, watching Rob out of the corner of her eye. Most men wouldn't be caught dead in that department.

"Okay."

"Are you going with me?"

"Of course. I told you I was going to stick to you."

She'd expected him to be nervous at shopping in that department. Instead he seemed perfectly at ease. *She* was the one who was uncomfortable.

"Doesn't this bother you?"

"Only when I start picturing you in some of these things," he told her with a smile that had heat in it.

Great! That was all she needed to upset her even more. She grabbed several panties and bras and a nightgown and marched over to the cash register. They were getting out of this department as soon as possible.

Once the underwear was in a generic shopping bag, Jessica's breathing returned to normal.

"Where to now?"

"I thought I'd buy a pantsuit and some more casual clothes. It will take a little longer, if you want to wait at a restaurant or shop in another department,'' she suggested.

''Nope, I'm staying with you. Since the engagement party is tonight, I don't want to risk your father finding you here. That could cause a major scene.''

She shuddered at the thought. ''But you don't even know what he looks like. How would you know if he came near us?''

''I remembered I've seen pictures of him, once you said who he was. We've never met, but I'd recognize him.''

''You never told me that.''

With a warm glint in his eyes, he reached out and stroked her cheek. ''We haven't known each other for even forty-eight hours, Jess. I've got to keep some secrets or you'll get bored with me.''

She caught his finger before she threw herself into his arms. The man's touch was devastating. ''You have too many secrets, Rob.''

Before he could answer, she was jostled by several women trying to reach a sales table. Releasing his finger, she forced herself to focus on her shopping. The sooner they were out of the store, the sooner she could put some distance between the two of them. And she desperately needed some distance.

The pricier clothing department had less of a crowd, and Jessica began to thumb through a rack of pantsuits. She'd expected Rob to wait in silence, but she discovered he intended to participate in her selection.

''I like that blue one. It would make your eyes stand out even more. Try it on.''

"But the blue is so bright," she protested.

"It wouldn't hurt to try it." He reached over her to take it off the rack. "I'll carry it for you until you're ready to try it on."

"Thanks," she muttered uneasily. When she stopped to look at a gray suit with clean lines, Rob offered his approval of it, also.

"Good one. Let's try it, too."

"Rob! You're not— I can shop by myself."

"I'm here. I might as well help."

As if his words had conjured her up, a saleswoman stepped up to them. "Good morning. I see you've already made some fine choices. May I put them in a dressing room for you?"

"Great," Rob agreed without consulting Jessica. He handed the two pantsuits over.

"I'll be right back if I can help you further," the woman said, beaming at Rob.

"Humph. I think I'm getting excellent service because she's flirting with you." Jessica wished she hadn't spoken since she realized her words showed a certain amount of jealousy.

"It's okay. I prefer you," Rob assured her with a teasing grin.

"That's not what— Never mind!"

"Try this dark green outfit. It might look good on you."

"Did you shop with your wife?"

"Sylvia? Nope. Never did."

"Then why are you so intent on helping me?"

"You don't like me to help you?"

"I don't— I'm not used to— Fine, I'll try on the

green one." How could she explain that the intimacy of their shopping together was making it more and more difficult to keep him at a distance?

"Anything else?" the saleswoman asked, at Rob's elbow again.

"Just this one," Jessica told her. "Where did you put the other two?"

"Right this way. We have some chairs where you may wait right outside the dressing rooms, sir, in case your wife wants to show you how they look."

"Great. I can't wait to see them on her," he said with a smile at the saleswoman, but then he turned that smile on Jessica, inviting her to play along.

She wanted to tell the saleswoman that he wasn't her husband, that he wasn't a nice man, but she said nothing. She wanted all those things too much.

Rob took a seat right outside Jessica's dressing room. "Would you like me to help you change, honey?"

Was it just for the benefit of the saleswoman? Jessica didn't know. Modulating her voice, she called back, "No, thank you, dear. I'll manage."

Once the door closed, leaving her alone, Jessica slumped down into the chair. Normally she enjoyed shopping, but this morning's outing seemed fraught with tension. Wanting to get it over with, she stood and removed her clothes. She'd just reached for the first pantsuit when the dressing room door opened.

Jess assumed the saleswoman had returned to offer her help. But a curious flutter she suddenly felt in her stomach made her look up. The person in the dressing room with her wasn't the saleswoman.

It was Rob.

Chapter Ten

Jessica let out a shrill shriek and clutched a jacket to cover herself. "What are you doing?" she screamed.

"Shh!" Rob cautioned even as his hand came over her mouth, giving her no choice but to remain silent. "Um, it's getting crowded out there," he whispered into her ear. "I thought you wouldn't mind if I—"

She pulled away. "Of course I mind. I don't know—"

He covered her mouth with his hand again. "Sssh, we don't want anyone to hear you."

"Why not?"

She wasn't a dummy, and Rob watched her thought processes take her to the natural conclusion. "Who's out there? My father?" she whispered.

He'd been undecided about what to tell her. He didn't mind sullying the reputation of the man she'd been engaged to, but he didn't want to hurt her if he didn't have to.

He shook his head. When she continued to stare at him, he mouthed the word, "Stephen."

She stared at him, questions in her gaze, then she whirled around to peer out the slats in the louvered door.

Rob enjoyed the view, since her back was to him, covered only with her bra and bikini panties. When she looked over her shoulder and caught his heated gaze, she gasped. Turning to face him, the jacket between them again, she glared at him even as she listened to the conversation outside the door—a conversation between Stephen Cattaloni and a female companion.

"Whatever you want, baby. Just pick it out."

"Ooh, Stevie, you're so generous."

"It's my nature."

"I still don't see why you have to get engaged to that woman tonight."

"I told you, baby. It's just for show. She's got a lot of connections I can use."

As Rob watched, Jessica's eyes narrowed, and anger filled her face. Not that he blamed her. Cattaloni was using her all the way. Now she had complete proof of it.

Fortunately he read her mind and leaped to her side to prevent her from opening the door. "No!" he whispered.

"I want to face him. I want his 'friend' to know that she can have him," Jessica whispered, breathing fire. "I want to tell him that I wouldn't marry him if he was the last man on earth."

"Jess, you need to talk to your father first. You don't know what hold Cattaloni has on him."

Since she was once more in his embrace, his

hands sliding across that silken skin, she didn't have to look far to question him. "You mean you don't want Stephen to see you, don't you? That's why you rushed in here. Not to warn me."

He shrugged his shoulders. "It was a combination of the two. It would be better for Cattaloni not to recognize me for a while. The company needs time to work someone else into the group before they become suspicious. But the most important thing was I didn't want you coming out to show me your new outfit and running into him." He ran his hands down her back, enjoying the feel of her.

"I have to get dressed," she protested, pushing him away. "Go over to the corner and turn your back."

"I'll stay here by the door and listen to your old pal while you get dressed," he promised. When she moved away from him, he reluctantly drew his gaze to the louvered door. The rustling sounds that came from her corner tested his resolve, but he didn't peek.

Once she had the gray pantsuit on, she came back to the door and he admired the sleek lines of her outfit. "Nice," he praised, running a finger down the collar.

"Is he still there?" she whispered.

"Yeah. Apparently, the lady wants a lot of gifts to make up for tonight."

"So we're trapped in here until they leave? The saleswoman will get suspicious— Oh, no, what will she say when she finds you in here?"

Rob couldn't resist her closeness. He pulled her

against him and covered her lips with his. Their soft, full warmth, melding to his lips, had him over the top in no time. His hands began unfastening the jacket, desperate to caress her soft skin.

"Rob." She said his name in a breathless voice, from outrage or desire he couldn't tell. But she didn't back away. His lips traced her jawline, savoring the taste of her, while his hands traced her back and over her breasts, relishing the feel of her. If he wasn't careful, he'd lose control again. Left to him, they'd be on the floor in thirty seconds flat.

A dressing room probably wasn't the best place for making love, especially for the first time, but he'd been a gentleman for forty-eight hours. With Jessica, he thought he might have reached his limit.

"We—we've got to stop this."

"Stop what?" he murmured, his lips reaching her neck. When she arched against him, his pulses leaped.

The annoying whine of Cattaloni's girlfriend interrupted, bringing both of them to a standstill.

"Tell me you want me, not her," the woman pleaded.

"Always, baby. She's a cold fish."

Rob, holding that cold fish in his arms and feeling ready to explode, grinned at Jessica.

"Does she turn you on, like I do?" the woman asked, her breathing heavy.

"No one turns me on like you. Come on, enough shopping, let's go back to bed."

"I think I need something shiny…like a diamond, before we leave."

"Sure, baby, sure. We'll drop by the jewelry department on the way out," he promised, his voice growing fainter.

Jessica eased the door open slightly and both of them peeked out to see the pair moving toward the escalator. Jessica closed the door and turned to him, leaning against it. "Now, as soon as they're gone, you've got to slip out. Then I'll finish trying on the outfits and we can go."

"Are you going to buy the one you're wearing? I like it." The jacket was still open, offering him a glimpse of the tops of her creamy white breasts. He'd like it even better if it were off her, lying on the dressing room floor, with the two of them stretched out on top of it. He drew a deep breath, trying to halt his runaway imagination.

"Probably," she said distractedly, turning to peek out the door once more. She faced him again. "I think they're gone. Why don't you—"

The door shoved against her back. "Hello, in there. Do you need any help, or other sizes?" the saleswoman called.

"No! No, I'm fine. And I'm very modest so don't...I'll let you know if I want anything."

"All right, dear. Your husband left, by the way."

"Yes, he had some shopping to do on his own."

Jessica slumped against the door and glared at Rob. "Look at the mess you've gotten us into. What if she sees you sneaking out?"

"She'll think we were enjoying ourselves."

"Rob! No one would—would they?"

"I've heard it happens. Not classy people like us,

of course, but there are those who don't care where they are." Like him when he touched her, he thought.

Groaning, Jessica turned and eased the door open again. "The coast is clear. Hurry up."

He slipped through the door and returned to the chair he'd earlier occupied before the saleswoman turned around.

When she saw him, she hurried over. "Your wife is still in the dressing room."

"Ah. Thanks for letting me know. She always takes a lot of time." He could imagine Jessica grinding her teeth at his words.

Either to prove him wrong, or because she was really fast, Jessica appeared only a couple of minutes later.

"Did any of them work for you?" the saleswoman eagerly asked.

"Yes, I'll take these."

Rob handed the woman a credit card.

"What are you doing?" Jessica said with a gasp, moving closer to him. "I'm paying for my clothes."

"I thought maybe you wouldn't want to use your credit card in case they notified your father."

She threw him an irritated glare. "I don't care if he knows I'm back in Kansas City. He won't know where to find me, thanks to you." She turned and hurried after the saleswoman. "Please charge them to *my* account. My friend needs his card back."

"Oh, I'm sorry. I assumed you were—I mean, most men only shop with their wives."

Rob couldn't pass up an opportunity to tease Jessica. "I'm getting in some practice for when we're married." The saleswoman beamed at him and Rob discovered he liked the idea of marrying Jessica. She didn't seem so pleased with his words.

"Are you determined to cause problems?" she whispered.

He grinned but said nothing in response. "Is that everything you need to buy?"

"No, I need shoes and some makeup."

"We'd better try another store. I don't want to run the risk of bumping into Stephen again," he warned her and took her packages from her.

JESSICA LEANED BACK against the leather upholstery of Rob's car and let the tension drain out of her. The shopping trip had been nerve-racking. For many reasons. Not the least of which was the handsome man beside her.

"I think I should talk to Dad today."

The words that sprang from her lips surprised her almost as much as Rob.

"No way. Remember? The party is tonight. You said you'd wait until tomorrow so he couldn't announce the engagement."

"But I've been thinking. When I tell him Stephen is connected to the mob and has a mistress, he won't want me to marry him. That'll keep him from announcing the engagement tonight. He can tell everyone I'm sick."

"He would do that? Announce it anyway?"

"Maybe." She wanted desperately to give her father one more chance. To prove to her that her suspicions about his behavior were wrong. It seemed she still wanted her father's belief in her.

"But if you call him from the house, he'll come after you."

"I could call him from a pay phone." She turned and stared at Rob, pleading with her eyes, begging him to understand. "He's my father. I have to give him another chance."

"He might track you down there."

"But that would take a while, wouldn't it?" She gnawed on her bottom lip as she thought. "I could tell him I'll come home tomorrow if he doesn't announce the engagement."

Rob pulled over and parked beside a pay phone at the edge of the Plaza. "Okay, call him. But limit yourself to two minutes. He'll probably send someone to find you."

Jessica was relieved when Rob remained in the car, after offering her a quarter. She refused, pulling one out of her purse. Then she crossed the sidewalk to the phone. After putting in the coin, she dialed her home number with shaky fingers.

"Dad, it's Jessica," she said as soon as he answered. Cutting through his demand that she come home at once, she said, "I've only got a minute. I want you to know that Stephen has mob connections and a mistress. I don't know how deeply you're involved with him, but I will never marry him, no matter what happens tonight."

"What are you saying?" he roared.

"You heard me."

"How do you know these things?"

"I know about the mob connection through a—a friend. And I observed Stephen with a young woman in Hall's and listened to him discussing his engagement to me as something he had to do for the 'connections.'"

"I can't believe it."

"Dad, I need to know. Are you doing anything illegal with Stephen?"

"No! Of course not. How could you think—"

"The company suddenly improved just after you became friends."

"He made me a loan. I told you that."

"You have to pay it back at once."

"I can't, Jessica. We're broke. I don't have the money to pay him back."

"Dad, if you don't, he's going to involve you in some unsavory shenanigans. I think he's setting you up for a money laundering scheme."

"I'd refuse."

"Then he'd call in your loan."

There was dead silence. Jessica could almost hear her father's panic building.

"Jessica, you must be mistaken."

"Promise me you won't announce the engagement tonight."

"Will you come home?"

"Tomorrow, if you don't make the announcement."

"I want you home now."

Rob touched her shoulder and she almost jumped out of her skin. He pointed to his watch.

"How much did you borrow from Stephen?" she hurriedly asked.

"I don't think I need to tell you—"

"How much?"

"A million dollars." There was a tightness in his voice that told Jessica how much he hated making that admission. Her heart sank as she took in the amount.

"I have to go, Dad. We'll talk tomorrow, work something out. Try to avoid a showdown with Stephen tonight."

"Yes, I'll—"

Rob hung up the phone for her.

"How dare you!" she exclaimed. "He was still talking."

"Get in the car before someone shows up here and follows us," he ordered, his voice firm. "I don't want any trouble for my kids."

The mention of Cathy and Michael worked much better than his orders. She didn't want to bring harm to those two, even though she couldn't see how talking another minute to her father would do so. For those two, she wouldn't take chances.

Rob eased his car away from the curb, pulling into the stream of traffic. Instead of heading back to the house, however, he made the block. Just ahead of him, a car Jessica recognized as one belonging to her father's assistant screeched to a halt beside the telephone she'd been using.

"Maybe you should duck down," Rob suggested, his gaze on the man who jumped out of the car.

Jessica did so as the man turned his head in their

direction, scanning all the cars parked along the road.

"What's he doing?" she whispered, hating that she couldn't watch, too.

"He's concentrating on people walking on the sidewalk and parked on the street. So far he's not looking at the cars moving along. But don't raise your head," he added sharply as she began sitting up.

"But I want to see."

"I don't want him trailing us, and if he sees you, he will."

"How did you know that my father would send someone?"

"Even if he believes you, he's too hardheaded to let you beat him at this game. It's my guess that he's angry that you escaped his control and caused him a lot of effort and embarrassment."

"You're pretty good at figuring people out."

"And it's my bet that he doesn't believe you about Stephen yet. What did he tell you?"

"He promised he's not doing anything illegal...yet. But since I'm learning how to think these things through after hanging out with you, my bet would be that Stephen's setting him up. He made him a million-dollar loan. Dad says he can't pay it back."

"Ah."

"Yeah, I'm sure his next step is to ask Dad to launder money with an offer to erase part of his debt to him. Right?"

"That's how they work sometimes." He checked

his rearview mirror as he turned onto a small street that bordered a park.

"Where are we going?"

"No place in particular. I just want to be sure we're not being tailed." He turned and smiled at her. "I'm being extra careful. What are you going to do now?"

"Figure out a way to pay off the loan."

He raised one eyebrow. "You've got that kind of money?"

"No. I've got a trust fund with half that amount. But paying off half of it wouldn't do much good, would it?"

"I'm afraid not."

"Then the house will have to go."

He frowned, pulled the car over to the side of the road and looked at her. "Your home?"

She nodded, not speaking. The thought of losing her home, where she'd spent her happy childhood, upset her. It was a large sprawling house and, under her mother's guidance, it had always been a home, a warm, welcome place where she could relax, bring her friends. After her mother's death, some of the heart had gone out of it, but it was still home.

"Will it bring enough money?"

"I think it's worth about three quarters of a million. I'll make up the rest from my trust fund."

"Will your father agree to selling his home?"

"Actually, I own half of it. Mother died without a will. I'm not going to give Dad an option. Selling the house is better than being indebted to a criminal."

"Cattaloni isn't going to like this. If he gets wind of it, he'll try to block the sale, or force the issue before you can arrange one. How long do you think it will take to find a buyer?"

Jessica buried her face in her hands. "I don't know. I'll have to talk to someone, find out. It's a beautiful home, but someone with that much money doesn't come along very often."

"Where is it?"

"Just off Ward Parkway, on the Missouri side. It's an old house, but Dad's had it modernized. There's a big yard, a pool, a five-car garage."

"How many bedrooms?"

She gave a watery chuckle. "You sound like a prospective buyer."

He grinned and pulled the car back onto the road. "Give me directions. I want to see this place."

She told him where to turn. They were only a few blocks away from it. When they approached it, she ducked down again. "I'd better hide. Someone might be watching for my dad's assistant to return."

"Right. It's huge, isn't it?"

"Oh, yes. But it's warm and welcoming, not like— I'm sorry. I shouldn't have said that."

"Don't worry. I know Sylvia's house is like a palace, cold and untouchable. That's why I want to find my own place." He drove slowly by the house. "You never said how many bedrooms."

"I'm not sure. I guess eight or nine. I converted the room next to my bedroom into a sitting room, and several others were divided into bathrooms when they redid the plumbing."

"It doesn't have a bowling alley, does it?"

"A bowling alley?" Jessica asked in surprise. She was bent over, her head resting on her knees. "Do you think a bowling alley would help it sell?"

"Nope. That would be too much. That's why I was asking. I've seen houses on television that have one. I think the White House has one in its basement."

"Our home isn't the White House. It's really very comfortable." She finished with a sigh.

"You can raise your head now."

"Did you like it?" she asked, watching him.

"Yeah, it looks great. Did you have a happy childhood?"

"Yes. My mother was alive until my senior year. After that, life wasn't so grand, but Dad and I have been very close. Until Stephen came along."

They drove in silence until she decided she wanted to know about his past, too. "Did you have a happy childhood?"

"Yeah, a great one. But my parents were killed in a plane crash my junior year in college. A bomb on the plane."

"Oh, no! Is that why— I mean, if you really did work for the FBI, is that why?"

"You believe me?"

She shrugged her shoulders. Maybe it was because she wanted so badly to believe him, but suddenly she did. "Yes, I guess I do. You're not at all like Stephen."

"Thank you. I would've been offended if you'd

thought we were alike." He leaned over and gave her a quick kiss.

She tried to dismiss the warmth that filled her at his touch. "So, was that the reason you went into the FBI?"

"That and the fact that I had no close family. It made me an ideal candidate. That fact also prompted me to marry Sylvia. After five years of being alone, I wanted a connection."

"You certainly found one. Three, I guess, counting Cathy and Michael."

"Yeah, which brings me back to my immediate problem. I have to find a place for us to be a family."

Jessica sighed again, thinking of her own home, where once they'd been a family. "Yes. Have you started looking?"

"I contacted a Realtor and he showed me some houses, but nothing I was interested in."

"Well, it takes time."

"I don't know. I think I've just solved my problem."

"Oh, really?"

"Yeah, I think I'll buy your house."

Chapter Eleven

Jessica stared at her companion in shock.

"Bad idea?" he asked gently. "If it will bother you, I won't—"

"No, no, I wouldn't mind, Rob, truly, but the price will be at least seven hundred and fifty thousand."

"I know."

She continued to stare at him. He turned the corner and caught her look. "What?"

"I—I'm a little confused. I mean, when I first met you, you were in a cabin in the woods, with one bathroom. I thought you were a criminal. Now, I can accept that you worked for the FBI, but you're wealthy? I didn't know we paid our agents that much."

He grinned. "Believe me, we don't."

"Then how can you even consider buying that expensive a house?"

He sighed and ran his hands over the steering wheel. "My family has had a lot of property, particularly in Chicago. When my grandfather sold some of it, it was in downtown Chicago, and he made a hefty profit.''

"Downtown Chicago?" she repeated faintly.

"Yeah. Lucky investment, huh?" He didn't mention the other things he'd inherited. His net worth meant he'd never have to work. But he would. And he hoped Jessica would understand.

"Yeah. Lucky." She didn't ask any more questions, turning to look out the window.

"So when can I see your house? I'd like to take the kids with me. I want them to like whatever I buy." The sooner this transaction took place, the sooner they could get settled. And then, something that was becoming more urgent every day, he intended to settle things with Jessica.

Things. A funny way to phrase the burning need that was growing in him.

He realized she hadn't answered him. "Jess?"

"I have to talk to my father first. Then I'll call you."

Her voice was so stiff that he turned to look at her again. "You're sure you're okay with me looking at it?"

"Of course. It'll be perfect. As I said, finding someone with that much money is hard to do. It would be stupid for me to turn down the opportunity to show you the house when I need a fast sale."

She stared straight ahead, her teeth sunk into her bottom lip, as he'd noted she always did when something was bothering her. He started to ask her what was wrong, but he decided he'd best wait until he wasn't driving. Picking up the phone, he dialed Mrs. Hutchins.

"We're on our way home. Hope you've got some lunch waiting for us."

After she promised to have food on the table when they arrived, he hung up the phone. "I hope you like roast beef sandwiches."

"No turkey?" she asked, assuming they'd be eating Thanksgiving leftovers.

"Nope. Mr. H. doesn't like turkey all that much. Since we were going to be gone, she cooked a big roast for the holiday."

"I like roast beef."

There was a decided lack of enthusiasm in her voice.

"If you want something else, all you have to do is tell Mrs. H. She's willing to do anything for you since you've been kind to the kids."

"I haven't done anything. They're terrific kids."

"Yeah." It pleased him that she liked his kids, but he was concerned about her sudden preoccupation. It had begun when he offered to buy her house.

When they reached home, after continuing the drive in silence, Cathy and Michael were waiting for them.

"Daddy, lunch is ready," Cathy announced as they scampered out the door to greet them.

"Good. Back inside. You don't have on a coat."

"Nana made cookies," Michael piped up, a big grin on his face.

"Then I guess you're happy, son," Rob said with

a smile. "Maybe a cookie will cheer up Jessica, too."

She turned to stare at him. "What makes you think I need cheering up?"

"Didn't you find anything to buy, Jessica?" Cathy asked at almost the same time. "Mommy always finds something to buy."

"Believe me, she found lots to buy," Rob teased, opening the car trunk. "Send Mr. H. out to help me carry all of it."

"I can—"

"No, go on inside with the kids," Rob ordered with a smile, dismissing Jessica's offer to help.

He stood watching as Cathy took her by the hand and pulled her into the house. Maybe the kids could erase that seemingly stricken look from her eyes. Certainly being with him hadn't done it.

DWELLING ON HER PROBLEMS seemed impossible around the children. Jessica knew she would have to face facts sometime soon. But not now.

After lunch, Rob suggested the kids put on outdoor clothes for a walk, so they could show Jessica around the neighborhood. Since he didn't ask if she wanted to go before he made the suggestion to Cathy and Michael, she could hardly tell them she wanted to mope in her room.

It would've wiped the joy from their faces.

"It's amazing that we could've been snowed in yesterday and today the temperature is so mild," she said as the four of them stepped outside, trying to concentrate on anything but her misery.

"There's still a definitive nip in the air," Rob assured her.

"What's a nip, Daddy?" Michael asked, a puzzled frown on his face.

"A little bite, Michael. It means you can feel the cold."

"A dog can nip you," Cathy added importantly. "Nana told me not to pet a dog I saw because it could nip me."

"Hey, I've been meaning to ask you guys about whether you wanted a dog," Rob said, taking Michael's hand while Jessica held Cathy's.

Michael's response was immediate. "Yes!"

Jessica noted Cathy's face lit up, then saddened. "We can't, Daddy. Mommy said she wouldn't have any animals in her house." She scuffed her shoes through a pile of leaves.

"But if I find us another house, with lots of room and a big yard, we wouldn't have to worry about that." Rob gazed at his daughter with such love in his eyes that Jessica had to turn away.

That's what she'd wanted from her father. That look, that belief that she was more important to him than anything material. Rob was the kind of father she'd always wanted. And that was another reason she knew he wasn't a bad guy. He was such a good daddy.

A look of wonderment spread over Cathy's face. "Really, Daddy? Really? We could have a dog?"

"We could, sweetheart. Would you like that?"

"Ooh, yes," Cathy said. "Wouldn't that be wonderful, Jessica?"

"Yes, sweetie, but a dog requires a lot of work, you know. You have to walk it, feed it, brush it," she reminded the little girl.

Her warning didn't take the shine out of Cathy's smile. "I'll do everything."

"Well, Michael could help, too," Rob added. "Unless we got two dogs, one for each of you."

Jessica couldn't help laughing. "You really like to jump in with both feet, don't you?"

There was a look in his eyes that took her breath away as he replied, "Yeah. I don't do anything half-heartedly."

He couldn't mean what she thought he meant. It didn't matter, even if he did. She knew that now.

"What kind of dog do you like, Cathy?" she asked hurriedly, hoping to distract herself from Rob's gaze.

The children's suggestions ran from a poodle to a Doberman. Rob persuaded them a Labrador might be a good compromise.

"A compromise to a toy poodle?" Jessica asked, not looking at Rob.

"Sure. Labs are sweet-natured, even if they are a little bigger."

"A little bigger? If a Lab sat in Cathy's lap, she'd be buried underneath."

Cathy's eyes grew round. "Are they as big as an elephant, Daddy?"

"I want an elephant!" Michael shouted, jumping up and down.

"Now look what you've done," Rob accused, staring at Jessica. But the grin on his face told her not to take him seriously. A good thing to remember.

"Can we go see one?" Cathy asked.

"Soon, baby, soon. We have to find a house first."

His gaze shifted back to Jessica, and she was reminded again of their earlier conversation. She'd had so many shocks lately. But maybe the biggest one of all was the revelation that she and her father could no longer consider themselves rich. And Rob could.

Which made any future between them impossible.

Rob's next words snapped her out of her misery. "I think I may have found us a house. Jessica's house."

"Jessica's house?" Cathy questioned. "You mean we could all live with Jessica?" Happiness filled her eyes.

"Oh, sweetie, no!" Jessica said, pain filling her.

"You don't want to live with us?"

Jessica stopped and knelt to pull Cathy into her arms. "It's not that. I think living with you and Michael would be a lot of fun. But I have to sell our house. I won't be living there."

"Then where will you live?" Cathy asked, cupping Jessica's cheeks with her little hands. "We'd share."

Abruptly standing, Jessica gave a wobbly smile to the child. Cathy's warm generosity only made things more difficult. "You are a sweetheart, but I can't. I'll find someplace else to live. Maybe close by and you and I can go shopping together some-times."

"Me, too," Michael said, realizing he was being excluded.

"Of course, Michael."

"Me, too."

Jessica whirled around to stare at Rob. "You—you can't—"

"You've already had your turn, Daddy," Cathy protested, interrupting, much to Jessica's relief.

"But it was a lot of fun. I want to go again."

He let his gaze roam over her, reminding her of when she'd caught him staring at her bare flesh. Shivers coursed through her, and she looked away.

"Anyway," she said breathlessly, trying to distract her audience, "if you buy my house, there'll be plenty of room for two dogs."

"And there's a swimming pool," Rob added.

"Yeah!" Michael enthused.

"Is there a room where I could keep my dollies?" Cathy asked.

"Oh, yes, Cathy. In fact, my rooms would be perfect for you, with a little redecoration. I have two rooms. You could keep your dolls and toys and books in one room, and sleep in the other." She thought back to the many hours of her childhood when she'd played in those rooms. "There's a comfy window seat that's perfect for reading when it's raining."

"But I'd be sad if I took your room," Cathy replied, a frown on her pretty face.

"No, don't you see? I'd be glad you were there

because I don't want my house to be sad. And it couldn't be if you and Michael were there.''

Cathy's brow cleared. "Oh. Okay. I've never had a window seat. Is it fun?"

"Oh, yes. It's great fun."

"Can I have one?" Michael asked.

Jessica shifted her gaze to Rob briefly and then away. "Your daddy could have one built, maybe."

"Okay," Michael agreed without ever questioning his father's willingness. Suddenly he dropped his father's hand and ran ahead. "Look, it's our hill!"

"Our hill?" Jessica repeated, puzzled.

"Daddy taught us how to roll down it," Cathy assured her excitedly. "Come on." She ran after Michael.

Rob's arms came around Jessica, startling her.

"You did a nice job reassuring Cathy," he whispered in her ear. "Thanks."

She pushed out of his hold. "No problem. I meant what I said." She also needed to keep some space between them. Rob's wont to touch her whenever he was in range wasn't helping her difficulties.

"Mad at me?" he asked, coming around to stare into her eyes.

"No, of course not. Cathy's calling us." She hurried down the sidewalk, leaving him to follow.

Cathy, with leaves in her hair and on her clothes, was at the bottom of a small hill, waving at them. "Look, Jessica, I rolled down the hill. Come on!"

"Me, too. I'm goin' again," Michael said as he charged back up the slope.

Jessica watched the children, a smile on her lips. Their enthusiasm was contagious.

"Well?" Rob prodded. "Aren't you going to roll down the hill?"

She looked at him with startled eyes. "Me?"

"Have you ever done it?"

"No."

Moving closer, he whispered, "Ah, a virgin!"

"Rob!"

"Kids, Jess has never rolled down a hill before," he called to his children.

"Don't worry, Jessica," Cathy returned. "Daddy will help you."

Jessica stared at Rob suspiciously. Somehow, she thought Cathy's response was exactly what Rob had expected. "What does she mean?"

"We'll roll together," he told her, his eyes twinkling with anticipation.

Before she could even think about his response, he'd pulled her to her knees, wrapped her arms around his waist and then started rolling down the hill.

By the time they reached the bottom, she had no breath left. Which was just as well because she would've lost it again. Lying in the dead leaves, she stared into Rob's eyes as he lay atop her, his warmth covering her from head to toe.

"Don't you think you should've warned me?" she asked, her breath coming in gasps.

"About what? Rolling down the hill? Or our...togetherness?"

"We're not together, Rob. And we can't be." She

tried to keep her voice casual, as if her statement hadn't shattered her dreams. But her father had taught her too well about the importance of money. Or lack thereof. She didn't want Rob to think she was influenced by his wealth.

He reared up so he could see her face clearly. "How can you say that when we're together right now. And I think it's fun."

Fun? He called this breath-stealing closeness fun? Jessica opened her mouth to tell him fun was an inadequate word for their touching and had no place in her future since it didn't include him. Before she could speak, Cathy interrupted.

"Did you like it?" the little girl asked, bending over them.

Slowly Rob raised himself off of her. "Yeah, Jess, did you like it?" He offered her a hand up.

Reluctantly she placed her hand in his and let him help her. "Uh, yes, it was...thrilling," she said, looking at Cathy, hoping Rob didn't know she was referring to his embrace rather than the roll.

"Now you can try it on your own," Cathy assured her, tugging her hand to follow her up the hill.

"I think she probably needs me to help her one more time," Rob said.

Without even looking at him, in case he tempted her too much, she followed Cathy. "Oh, no, I don't think so. I can do it by myself."

She was going to have to do a lot of things alone from now on.

"TODAY WAS SO FUN," Cathy said, leaning against Jessica as she sat on the sofa in the den. The little girl put her arms around Jessica's neck and hugged her. "Thank you for playing with us."

"I had fun, too, Cathy."

Michael crawled up in his father's lap. "I'm tired."

"We must've really worn you out, son. Come on, I'll help you to bed."

"Want me to put him to bed?" Mrs. Hutchins asked, laying down her knitting needles.

"No, I'll take care of him," Rob said, lifting Michael into his arms. The little boy's head rested confidently on his father's shoulders. "Tell everyone good-night, Michael."

"Night-night," the little boy muttered sleepily.

"Are you ready for bed, too, Cathy?" Jessica asked.

"No. I'm not sleepy. But will you put me to bed when I'm ready?"

Jessica quickly looked at Mrs. Hutchins, afraid Cathy's request would hurt her feelings. But Mrs. Hutchins smiled at Jessica, with no displeasure in her eyes.

"If your father doesn't mind."

"He won't mind," the older lady assured her. "I suspect he'll be pleased."

Jessica didn't want to think about Mrs. Hutchins's words. Maybe she should rethink taking Cathy to bed.

With Mr. Hutchins gone into the kitchen momentarily, and Rob and Michael upstairs, Mrs. Hutchins smiled at Jessica and added, "That boy's a natural father."

Jessica didn't have to ask who the woman was talking about. "Yes, he is."

"He was worried, you know."

"About what, Nana?" Cathy asked.

"Whoops, I forgot about little ears. Your daddy was worried he wouldn't know how to be a daddy, since he was away so much."

"That's silly, Nana. Of course, he's our daddy. He has to know how."

Jessica hugged her. "That's good, 'cause I think he's a very good daddy."

"Yeah, the best." Cathy returned the hug.

Mrs. Hutchins laughed. "And if he didn't know how, he'd work hard learning. When he was little, he'd keep trying till he got something right. He's so stubborn."

Jessica nodded. Mrs. Hutchins was right. Rob was no quitter. Even if he hadn't inherited money, he'd probably be successful. She wondered what he'd do with himself now that he'd quit his job. "Mrs. Hutchins, has Rob discussed his plans with you? I mean, isn't he going to miss work?"

"Well, I think he'll figure out something to do. But I'd rather he not be doing such a dangerous job."

She could agree with that opinion. The thought of Rob being injured, or even killed, chilled Jessica's heart. He was so warmhearted, and touched those he loved so much, it didn't bear thinking about.

With Cathy's arms still around her, Jessica realized she'd had more hugs, some more exciting than others, in the past two days than she had had in years. They felt good.

"Hey, no fair doing all this hugging when I'm gone," Rob protested, coming back into the den. "I don't want to be left out."

Jessica stood abruptly. "I was, uh, hugging Cathy good-night."

He stared at her before looking to his child.

"You ready for bed, pumpkin?"

"I guess," Cathy agreed reluctantly. Jessica thought she was going to escape her promise, but Cathy remembered.

"But Jessica promised to tuck me in."

"I think maybe your dad should have the honor tonight, Cathy," Jessica hurriedly said. "Another time I'll tuck you in."

"I don't think Jessica has a lot of experience with tucking in, pumpkin. She'll probably have to practice on big people before she can be trusted to tuck you in."

His knowing look told her the exact meaning of his words.

Mrs. Hutchins chuckled at Rob's teasing, but Jessica ignored him as best she could. Since her cheeks were hot, she didn't think she did a very good job, but she wasn't going to look at him.

He swept Cathy into his arms and carried her upstairs.

"Don't let him bother you," Mrs. Hutchins said, as her husband came into the room. "He loves to tease."

"Are you talking about me?" Mr. Hutchins demanded.

"No, you big silly. I was talking about Rob."

Her husband nodded. "Yeah, he does like to tease. But he's a good boy."

The two spoke as if they were his parents. Though they were employed by Rob, they were treated as family.

She'd been fond of some of the people who worked for her family, but she'd never had closeness like this. Maybe if she had, she wouldn't have been so lonely growing up. That loneliness was also the reason she'd always vowed she'd have more than one child.

Now she wasn't sure she'd ever have children. Because the man she'd fallen in love with might not be interested in someone outside his...financial neighborhood. That's what her father had taught her.

"What are you thinking about, Jessica?" Rob asked, as he came back into the room.

"Nothing! Why?"

"You looked sad."

"I—I was thinking about this evening. I never had anyone to share the nights with. I mean, unless I had friends over."

He smiled at her. "We'll be glad to be your family," he said, gesturing to the two older people. They both nodded with smiles.

She didn't know what to say. It would be wonderful to take them up on that offer. But she didn't think it would be possible.

Before she could work out a polite response, Rob

spoke again. "Don't go anywhere, young lady. I'm going to lock up and then I'll be right back."

"What is it? Do we need to talk?" Did he have more revelations? She didn't think she could handle much more.

"Nope. No more talking. You promised later, and later has finally arrived."

Mr. and Mrs. Hutchins suddenly said good-night and hurried from the room.

Chapter Twelve

Jessica's entire body suffused with color as she took in Rob's words. He was talking about hugging. She whipped her head around, trying to decide if she could escape as the Hutchinses had.

If Rob was as fast with the locks as he'd been with the children, she'd have to run to reach her room. And run she would. She couldn't afford to have Rob's charms unleashed.

Not now.

She had just started up the stairs when Rob caught her arm and pulled her around against his hard chest.

"Oh!"

His arms captured her.

"I had no idea you'd be eager enough to jump on me," he teased and dipped his head to kiss her.

She turned her face away. "No! I mean, I'm not. It's late and I thought I'd go to bed. Alone!" she gasped, not wanting any misunderstanding.

"Really? Ten o'clock is your normal bedtime?" he asked, continuing to hold her against him.

"I—it's been a long day."

"Okay. If you don't want to play, we might as well talk," he said, a serious look filling his features.

Her heart lurched as she considered his words. "You have something else to tell me?" In spite of herself, her voice wavered.

His hands ran up and down her arms as he smiled at her. "Nope, no more bombshells. At least, I don't think so. But I thought we should make sure you understand—well, how serious this business could get." His smile was gone now.

"I told Dad not to say anything to Stephen," she protested. "As long as he has no idea we're on to him, everything will be all right, won't it?"

"Are you sure your father will do as you asked?"

"Of course, he—he—" She broke off, remembering the few times in the past she'd tried to persuade her father to a certain course of action. "I think so. But I might be more assured of it if you hadn't hung up the phone."

"And your father's assistant would've caught you on the phone if I hadn't," he reminded her.

"I forgot."

He turned her around, sloping one arm around her, and started down the stairs. "That's why I think we need to talk. Have the Hutchinses gone to bed?"

"Yes." Which meant, of course, that they'd be all alone downstairs. The one thing she'd meant to avoid. But he seemed impossible to resist.

They returned to the kitchen and he pulled out a chair at the table for her. "I'll put on some coffee."

"It might keep us up," she hurriedly said. She didn't need any more stimulation.

"It's decaf. No problem."

Jessica sighed. No problem. Rob always seemed to have an answer, but he didn't understand Jessica's problems. Particularly when he was at the center of them.

"By the way, both kids told me how much fun they had today," he said as he filled the carafe with water.

"It was fun," she said, trying to keep the wistfulness she felt from her voice. "But we didn't do much."

"I think those times are more fun than planned activities. Do you know the kids hadn't rolled down a hill until I taught them last week?"

"I hadn't, either."

"I know. I think rolling down a hill, playing in the leaves, having a puppy—those are essential parts of childhood. Did you have a puppy?"

"No. My father doesn't like animals in the house."

Rob shot her a sharp look but said nothing.

As if he'd criticized her father, she protested, "Lots of people don't like animals in the house."

"So you never had any pets?"

She didn't like his question. It reminded her of the longing she'd felt as a child, wanting a puppy to cuddle and share things with. She was grown up now. She'd gotten over such silliness, hadn't she? "I had a goldfish once. But it died."

He snorted in disgust. "You can't pet a goldfish."

"I know."

She hadn't realized he'd moved until he touched

her shoulder. "You can go with us to pick out the puppies."

No, she couldn't, as much as her heart wanted to agree. "Thanks, but I'll probably have to work." Now more than ever.

"We'll go in the evening, then."

Jessica remained silent. What was the point of arguing, anyway? Once she'd convinced her father to sell their home to Rob, she wouldn't see him or the children again. She couldn't.

All her life she'd been warned about other people using her, pursuing her, because of her family's wealth. It had made it difficult to have friends, unless they were handpicked by her father. It had made it almost impossible to consider marriage.

When she found Rob and his children, Jessica had begun to think she'd found someone she could trust, someone who might like her without knowing she was wealthy.

Then came the shock of discovering she was no longer wealthy. But Rob was. He wouldn't want to marry someone who wasn't in his class. And her pride wouldn't allow her to even if he was interested.

"Jessica?"

"What?"

"Where'd you go? I've been talking, but you haven't been listening."

"What did you say?"

He sat down in the chair beside her. "I asked if you enjoyed rolling down the hill."

Her body tightened as she remembered being

wrapped in his arms, landing at the bottom of the hill, touching his strong frame from her head to her toes.

Oh, yes, she'd enjoyed it. Too much.

"Yes, it was fun," she said politely, hoping to keep her voice calm.

He grinned. "I liked it, too. It's the most fun I've ever had rolling down a hill."

"Why?" She wanted to take back her question, knowing she shouldn't have asked it.

"Because I was holding you," he whispered and reached for her. His lips covered hers and he pulled her body against him. Her hands splayed against his chest, intending to keep him at a distance, but her fingers ignored her command, loving the feel of his muscles beneath them.

His lips teased and cajoled, caressed and tortured until, with a sigh, she surrendered, opening her mouth to him. Her arms slid around his neck and she pressed against him.

Before she even realized his intent, Rob scooped her out of her chair and into his lap. She would've protested, she felt sure, except that she was busy at the time. Her hands were unbuttoning his shirt, desperate to feel flesh against flesh, to surge through the dark hair that covered his chest.

For the first time in her life, Jessica wanted to forget everything but the man who held her. She wanted to be a part of him with a hunger that stunned her. Caressing him with total abandon, she made no protest when he pulled her shirt from her jeans and stroked her skin, too.

His mouth left hers to pursue a hot trail down her neck, leaving his brand on her skin. When he pulled her shirt over her head and released her bra, she pressed against his touch, not even bothered by her nakedness.

All she wanted was equal rights. She wanted to trace every inch of him. Excitement built in her so intensely, she thought she would explode. Then his lips reached her breasts and she almost fell apart. "Rob!"

"Shh, baby, it's all right," he whispered in return, then returned to her lips for more loving.

She became confused when he buried his face in her hair, one hand cupping her breast, and didn't move.

"Rob?"

"Don't move, Jess. I'm trying to control myself, but it's not easy."

"Control?" Did he mean the magic was over? That he didn't want her?

A rueful chuckle was his only response until she shifted against him. Then he spoke. "You do that again and I'll take you right here on the kitchen floor. Which could be a problem if the Hutchinses or one of the kids come down for a glass of water."

She gasped, suddenly realizing she was unclothed from her waist up. Shooting up from his lap, she began searching for her bra and shirt.

"Hey, where are you going?" he protested.

"I—I have to go upstairs."

He stood and wrapped his arms around her even as she pushed him away.

"Rob, turn me loose."

"Never," he said and kissed her neck, starting the adrenaline rush that his touch ignited. "Are you embarrassed about this?"

"Yes. I've never—never lost control in a kitchen."

"I'm glad I'm your first. The only problem is we're not alone here. We could go upstairs to my bedroom, but sometimes the kids come in if they have trouble sleeping."

She struggled to fasten her bra.

"Here, let me help."

As embarrassing as it was for him to dress her, at least it meant he wasn't holding her against him. She eased away as he snapped the closure and shrugged into her shirt.

"I like you better without your clothes," he assured her, a teasing grin on his face.

She couldn't answer him since his shirt hung open and she was greedily staring at it, wishing she could touch him again.

"I'll be on my way in the morning," she suddenly assured him. "If I don't see you—"

"Why wouldn't you see me?"

"You might—might sleep late or have something you need to do." She swallowed and looked away from him. She had to or she'd throw herself back into his arms. "I don't know your schedule."

"It's Saturday morning. I don't have a schedule on Saturday mornings. I'm at your command."

"I'm trying to say thank you for letting me stay here. It was very generous of you." It was absurd to talk to a man who'd just caressed the senses out of her as if he were a stranger, but Jessica was desperate to ignore what had happened.

"You're welcome." When she avoided his attempt to kiss her again, he looked at her sharply. "Are you all right?"

"Yes, of course. But things will change tomorrow. I'll go back home and—and you and the children—"

"I'm going with you."

His calm announcement startled her and left her in midsentence, her mouth hanging open. "What? I can't show you the house until after I've spoken to my father. I'll call you when—"

"That's not why I'm going. It's necessary that your father understand the seriousness of the situation. If not, he could put you and him in danger."

"I can explain it to him."

"That's just it, Jess. I'm not sure you can. From what I've gathered, your father seems hardheaded. He's not going to want to listen to you."

She crossed her arms over her chest and wished he'd button his shirt. "I'll make him."

"I'll come with you."

"No! I don't want you to."

"Hey, I can't abandon Goldilocks now. You're my responsibility."

"I am not. Goldilocks ran away from the three bears. She took care of herself."

He reached for her once more and held her against him, her folded arms trapped between them. "But I'm not the real bear, sweetheart. Stephen is. And this isn't a fairy tale. Someone could get hurt."

She knew that. But it wasn't Stephen who would hurt her. It was Rob, with his sexy body, his hot caresses, his darling children. She was falling in love with him, and she couldn't be a part of his life.

Kansas City society would embrace him whole-heartedly, the women in particular. He'd be the center of Jessica's world, the world she wouldn't be a part of. Without money, she knew she'd be ignored. She'd seen it happen before. At least she wouldn't have to watch while Rob found a wife, a new mother for Cathy and Michael.

But she'd know. And the pain would be intolerable.

"I have to go upstairs," she whispered and she tried to wrench herself from his hold.

"Jess, I want your promise."

"About what?"

"That I can go with you to see your father. I can't compromise on this issue."

"Compromise? When have you ever compromised?" she asked, her voice rising. Was hysteria setting in?

"Hey, I didn't make love to you on the kitchen floor. Believe me, that was a giant compromise."

And one she regretted. She thought she could bear telling him goodbye…maybe…if just once she could make love with him.

"I don't see the need for you to even meet my father. He won't be happy that you helped me escape him."

"All the more reason for me to be there, to take some of the heat off you."

He was offering to protect her, to be her hero. As if she needed more reasons to love him.

"Promise me, Jess."

"Why don't I go talk to Dad alone, and if I can't convince him, I'll call you." He wanted to talk compromise, so she offered him one.

"Nope. And don't even think about getting up early and sneaking out. I know where you live."

She pushed against him as she regretted showing him her house. But he would've found her anyway.

"Stop wriggling against me, or I'm going to take you to my bed, no matter who comes in."

In spite of what she'd like, she went stone still. "Let me go, then."

"I'm going to. Soon. Because if I don't I'll die from frustration. We should wait until we get things cleared up with your father, anyway." He gave her a quick kiss that made her mouth water with longing.

"Daddy?"

Michael's plaintive call made them spring apart as they turned to face the four-year-old.

"Hi, buddy. Are you having trouble sleeping?"

"I had a bad dream, and you weren't in your room. Why were you kissing Jessica?"

"Because she's going up to bed and I was giving her a good-night kiss."

"Oh. Can I have some milk?"

Jessica was amazed that Michael bought his father's explanation, but she was grateful. Rob moved toward the refrigerator and she eased herself closer to the door. Here was her chance to escape, before she completely lost her mind.

"Wait, Jessica," Michael said, watching her. "I didn't get to kiss you good-night."

Unable to resist, she bent and held out her arms. Michael enthusiastically threw his arms around her neck and kissed her cheek. "'Night."

"Good night, Michael. I'll see you in the morning."

"Yeah. Can we roll down the hill again, Daddy? Jessica liked it, too."

"We'll see. Jessica and I may have to go visit her father in the morning."

"I have to go home, Michael."

"You're leaving? But aren't we going to your house?"

Jessica closed her eyes. Things just kept getting more and more complicated. "I'm not sure yet. Your daddy will explain in the morning. Good night," she added and ran for the door. Since Michael still had to drink his milk, she made her escape without either of the male Berensons catching her.

"WHY IS YOUR SHIRT unbuttoned, Daddy?" Michael asked as he accepted the glass of milk.

Rob looked down. He'd forgotten that Jessica had attempted to remove his shirt. Not that he'd objected, but he'd been otherwise occupied. And that occupation, as it replayed in his mind, didn't ease the tightness of his jeans.

"I'm getting ready to go to bed, too, son. Did your dream scare you?"

Michael, a milk mustache on his face, took down the glass and smiled at his father. "A little. But then I remembered how much fun we had today. That made me feel better. I want Jessica to stay with us."

Rob stared at his little boy. Out of the mouths of babes, he guessed. He should've realized before now. All along, he'd known he was in love with Jessica. Or headed in that direction. But he'd believed he had time. Time to decide whether or not she would be a part of them.

With an almost relieved chuckle, he said, "Me, too."

"She's lots more fun than Mommy."

Rob sighed. He couldn't let Michael knock his mother. "It's not easy being a mom, Michael. Your mom has taken good care of you."

"I know, but she doesn't like to play games or go for walks. She dresses up and goes shopping and things. Jessica wears jeans. And she hugs us and everything."

"Your mother hugged you."

"Only when we was clean. Nana and Papaw hug us lots more."

Rob couldn't argue with his son. He knew what he said was true. His ex-wife concentrated on her comfort and happiness more than anyone else's.

With a resolve that satisfied something deep within him, Rob said, "I'm going to do my best to convince Jessica to stay with us. Maybe she will."

"Yeah!" Michael tilted the glass up again and drained it. "Cathy loves Jessica, too."

"I know, son. We all do." It didn't even bother

Rob to admit to the emotion that filled him. An amazing happening. He'd thought it might take him some time before he could accept loving Jessica to the point that he wanted to marry her. He'd intended to keep his distance until he had settled into fatherhood, but now he realized he'd be as successful at holding back as he would at trying to dam up a river.

She was as much a part of him now as his children. Together they formed a family. A family that needed to be made legal. Because he wasn't letting anyone or anything come between him and his family.

Michael handed him the glass and then took his other hand in his. "It will be fun with Jessica. And the puppies. We can still have the puppies even if we get Jessica, can't we, Daddy?"

Rob chuckled. "Yeah, we can. You and Cathy can take care of the puppies, and I'll take care of Jessica. Okay?"

And thinking about taking care of Jessica meant he'd have a hard time getting to sleep tonight.

WHEN JESSICA finally awoke the next morning, her eyes felt as if the leaves she'd rolled in were in them. She'd lain awake until early morning, trying to come to terms with leaving Rob and his children.

She hadn't succeeded very well.

If only her father hadn't put them in such a difficult position. But she really couldn't put all the blame on him. He hadn't consulted her about his business decisions, but then she worked for him.

He'd never offered her any control or a vote in what happened there.

But she'd accepted Stephen, because she had almost given up on finding someone she could love. She'd allowed him to date her, to kiss her, to assume she was willing to go along with her father's plans. And she had been, until she found her mother's letters and had awakened, as if from a deep sleep.

And immediately fallen in love with Rob.

With a sigh, she shoved back the cover. It was already almost ten o'clock. Even though she hadn't gotten to sleep until four, she couldn't stay in bed any longer. As it was, Mrs. Hutchins was going to think she was lazy.

Maybe Rob would've already gone out, and she could eat and say her goodbyes without him around.

Yeah, right.

Half an hour later, dressed in the gray pantsuit she'd bought yesterday, she came down to the kitchen to discover Rob waiting at the table.

"Good morning, sleepyhead."

"I'm sorry, I didn't mean to sleep so late," she assured Mrs. Hutchins, ignoring Rob's cheerful smile.

"It's not that late, child. Sit down and I'll fix you some breakfast."

"I don't need—"

"Yes, you do. Mrs. H. fixed homemade cinnamon rolls this morning. You don't want to miss those." Rob pulled out the chair beside him.

Jessica licked her lips, suddenly yearning for the rolls, but she couldn't give in.

"They sound lovely, but I need to go back home. Thank you so much for—"

"You can't go."

She shifted her gaze from Mrs. Hutchins to the infuriating man beside her. "Of course I can. I told you last night—"

He didn't answer or interrupt her. He simply spread out the newspaper, turned to the society page.

Beneath a picture of her, her father, according to the words printed there, proudly announced her engagement to Stephen Cattaloni.

Chapter Thirteen

"No!" Jessica gasped.

Rob rose and put an arm around her, feeling her trembling beneath his touch. "Sit down, Jess. Mrs. H., pour her a cup of coffee and fix her some breakfast."

"I can't eat. I have to talk to my father. How could he?" she cried passionately. "I explained..."

He eased her down into the chair beside his and took her hand as he sat down. "Jess, maybe he didn't announce the engagement at the party last night. Maybe it was too late to cancel the announcement." He wasn't sure he believed that himself. Somehow, the picture that was becoming more clear each day was that of a selfish man who didn't deserve his daughter's love or concern.

A sigh rippled through Jessica. Feeling it, he wanted to hold her against him, to absorb the shock. Maybe he should've taken her upstairs to show her the paper.

No. He couldn't do that. He'd have her in bed in no time. It had almost killed him last night to let her go. But he didn't want his children to discover the two of them in an inappropriate—hell, in bed together. That wouldn't be responsible behavior in a parent.

"Do you think so?" she asked. Her blue eyes were filled with hope as she stared at him.

He had to work hard to remember what she could be asking. Finally he nodded his head. "It's possible. I think he would've had time to cancel it if he'd called at once yesterday, but he probably needed time to think."

"How will I know? And does that make any difference? Everyone is going to believe I'm engaged to that criminal, whether they announced it last night or not. I won't stand for it!" She pulled her hand away from him and covered her face.

He slipped his arm around her. "Now, Jess, we'll work it out. Come on, here's your breakfast."

Mrs. Hutchins had heated up a cinnamon roll and added strips of crisp bacon, orange juice and her cup of coffee.

"I don't know how you think we can work this mess out," Jessica protested even as she took a bite of cinnamon roll. Even in her distressed state, she stopped to praise Mrs. Hutchins's cooking. "These are wonderful."

"Thank you. I'm going to do laundry now. You call if you need anything else."

Rob waited until his housekeeper was out the door before he kissed Jessica. She immediately pulled away, not nearly satisfying the raging hunger he felt for her.

"Where are the children?"

"Out rolling down the hill with Mr. H. to supervise." He grinned at her. "You worried about being caught kissing me?"

"I don't think a good-night kiss would work as an explanation this morning," she said, looking away from him. But he was encouraged by her crimson cheeks.

"So I'll think of something else." He tried for another kiss, but she pulled back.

"I need to talk to my father."

He agreed with a sigh. He'd rather be kissing her. "I know you do. We'll go to another pay phone. Farther away this time so you'll have more than a couple of minutes to talk."

"I can take a taxi. You don't have to—"

"I told you last night I was going with you, Jess. I don't want any more arguing about it."

"You sound like Napoléon," she protested, folding her arms across her chest. "I'm not one of your loyal subjects waiting for your every command!"

"Eat your breakfast and stop pouting. It will be easier if I drive you to a pay phone." He got up to refill his cup from the coffeepot. "Mrs. H. couldn't figure out why there was a pot of coffee ready when she came down this morning."

His attempt to distract her worked as her cheeks flushed. "I forgot about it."

"Me, too. We had much more interesting things to do than to drink coffee." And he'd like to repeat every one of them and add a few more to the list.

She wouldn't look at him as her cheeks heated up

even more. Was she embarrassed? Or was she thinking like him?

Whatever was causing that reaction prompted her to eat her breakfast, which was all to the good. He didn't want her passing out on him.

He was concerned that her father would lie to her to get her to come back home. He wasn't sure how he could prove it, but Rob didn't trust John Barnes. It would be a real tightrope act to protect her without accusing her father of anything.

Remaining silent until she finished eating, he leaned against the cabinet, drinking his third cup of coffee and watched her. The gray pantsuit gave her a cool, sophisticated image, but he knew a warm heart—and some delightful curves—rested underneath. He wanted to claim her for his own.

And he would. Jessica Barnes was going to become a Berenson as soon as he could manage it. But first, they had to deal with her father.

"Ready to go?" he asked when she wiped her mouth with the napkin.

"Rob—"

"Don't even start. I'm taking you and that's final."

She didn't argue this time. But she sailed past him with her nose in the air, as if she never intended to speak to him again.

THE MAN WAS A TYRANT!

Jessica held herself stiffly in her seat in the Mercedes, refusing to relax against the soft leather. He thought he could be in charge of her life just because she'd hidden in his cabin in the woods.

After about ten minutes, she sagged against the seat, unable to maintain her rigidity.

"Good. I was afraid you'd stay mad at me all day," he teased, grinning at her, making it clear he'd been aware of her tension.

"I intend to. But it's too tiring to stay so tense."

"What have I done wrong?"

She glared at him. As if he didn't know! "You insist on having your own way. This is my problem, not yours."

Raising one eyebrow, he asked, "We're friends, aren't we? Don't friends help each other?"

His words pierced her heart, as if it were a knife. Friends? She'd almost given herself to him last night. Did he think that was friendship? Did he think she slept with anyone who gave her a kind word? "I think a friend should wait until he's asked for help."

"Nope. That won't do. You're so stubborn and proud, you'd never ask for help."

She sighed. He'd read her better than she'd thought. But she couldn't let him get any closer to her. "I don't want to put Cathy and Michael at risk."

"That's why we're going to a pay phone."

His response startled her. She'd given that excuse as an attempt to keep him at bay. "You don't really think—"

"Probably not. But I don't believe in taking foolish chances. Besides, you don't want him to know where you're hiding, do you?''

"No, though there's no real reason not to go home now," she said slowly, thinking about her situation. "I mean, I was only staying away so he wouldn't announce the engagement at the party. Now that the party is over—"

"What if he did announce it at the party? What are you going to do?"

"Send a retraction to the paper."

"What if Stephen is already threatening your father?"

She turned to stare at him, trying to judge his seriousness. "You don't believe that's true, do you?"

He shrugged his shoulders. "It's hard to tell. When you talk to him, if he says he didn't make the announcement, or that it was too late to cancel, tell him you're not coming home until you see a retraction printed."

"But, Rob, that could take several days." Which meant she'd become more involved with Rob and his family.

"You don't think we're going to kick you out, do you?" he asked, smiling at her. "The kids are begging you to stay forever."

The kids. Not him. Oh, he'd like her to grace his bed, but *he* certainly wasn't begging her to stay.

"But we both know that's not possible." She watched him out of the corner of her eye, just in case he showed any desire for her company.

"I guess not," he said casually, passing a slow car.

"Where are we going, anyway? Surely there are closer pay phones?"

"We're going to the airport."

"The airport? But that's forty-five minutes away."

"Right. It will give you time to talk to him without his being able to send someone to track you down."

"That's ridiculous, Rob. We don't need to go that far."

He ignored her and continued to drive.

"DAD, it's Jessica."

"Jessica! Where are you?"

"I'm sure your caller ID will tell you. Are you using a crisscross directory?" She figured that was how he found her yesterday so quickly. "Don't bother. I'm at the airport."

"You're leaving?"

"I don't know. Why was the announcement in the paper this morning?"

"It was too late to cancel it."

"Did you try?"

"Of course I did, dear. After what you told me, I wouldn't try to force you into a marriage with Stephen. Of course, I think you've judged him rather harshly."

"What did you tell him, Dad?"

"I told him you'd seen him with another woman and you were jealous."

"What?" She couldn't believe he'd say such a thing.

"Well, that's what it comes down to. Stephen didn't try to lie to me, Jessica. But he explained that he honored you too much to try to sleep with you before marriage. And a man does have needs, you know. He'll break it off with her as soon as the two of you are married."

Jessica bit down on her bottom lip until the pain almost made her cry out. "You haven't sent a retraction to the paper, have you, Dad?"

"How could I do that before you and Stephen have a chance to talk things through? I asked him if he'd call in the loan if you didn't marry him, and he assured me he wouldn't. After all, he made the loan as a friend."

Jessica felt Rob's hand on her shoulder. In spite of her intentions, she leaned into his warmth. Her body felt strangely chilled right now.

"Dad, didn't you hear me say Stephen has mob connections?" Frustration built as she waited for his answer.

"I told him you had doubts about his intentions, Jessica, but he assured me he'd loaned me the money to help out. I think you're getting carried away."

"And you'd rather believe a man you've known for a few months than your own daughter." A dull ache filled her. All the years she'd tried to be the son he wanted were worth nothing.

"Even if I did, I can't pay the man back," he protested testily.

"I've worked that out, Dad. We could sell the house. I've even found a potential buyer. I could pay the last quarter of the loan from my trust fund."

"Sell the house? You must be out of your mind. Everyone would know we had money difficulties. It would be unbearable."

Jessica closed her eyes. He didn't believe her, and he had no intention of getting out of the mess he was in.

"I'll be coming by the house either today or tomorrow to pack my things, Dad. If you could ask the housekeeper to get started on it, I'd appreciate it."

"Pack your things? Don't be ridiculous! You'll stay right here in your own home where you belong."

"No, I won't. I can't live there any longer."

"Then clear out your desk, too, while you're at it," he snapped.

She remembered Rob's words, that she would lose her job. She hadn't believed him. "You're firing me?"

"Damn right I'm firing you. You have no loyalty to me."

Jessica had to laugh at the irony of his words. "No, I guess I don't."

Without waiting for his response, she hung up the phone. It took several minutes to realize she was leaning back against Rob, his arms around her. It was hard to withdraw from his healing warmth, but she had to break away.

Trying for a smile, she failed miserably as she turned to face him. "I guess that's that."

"What did he say?"

"He doesn't believe me. He's taking Stephen's side."

"Did he accuse him of anything?"

"No, except having a mistress and loaning him the money for ulterior motives. He doesn't want to know," she admitted sadly.

"And selling the house?"

"It would be too embarrassing. I'm sorry, but I'm sure you can find a better place for Cathy and Michael. Now that I think about it, that's not a happy house."

"You're right. And we want a happy house. Ready to go to the newspaper office?"

Her mind still dwelling on her father's response, she stared at him, confused. "Why?"

"We need to place a retraction of the engagement."

She sighed. "You're right. Yes, thank you, I'd like to take care of that piece of business. Then I'll get out of your hair. I can go to a hotel tonight."

He smiled at her but didn't contradict her plans, and her heart, already pummeled by her father's behavior, sank even lower.

THOUGH IT HAD BEEN his idea that they go to the newspaper next, Rob stayed in the background, acting only as Jessica's escort. He sensed she needed to feel in control again. Her damned father had done enough damage for the day.

Of course, he didn't intend to let her go to a hotel. Unless he went with her. He almost laughed at that thought. He'd better control his urges until she caught her second wind. Otherwise he'd be taking advantage of her emotional turmoil.

When they came together, as they would, he assured himself, he wanted Jessica to want him as much as he wanted her. But not to need him to survive. Right now, she needed some support, not sex. And he was determined to provide what she needed.

"Thank goodness that's over," Jessica said as they left the newspaper building.

"Yep. You are now officially unengaged."

"Or I will be tomorrow when it appears in the Sunday paper. With the largest circulation," she added with satisfaction.

"Just to be on the safe side, we'll cut out the announcement and mail it to Stephen."

"That's a good idea. I'll do that."

He ignored her leaving him out of the plan. "How about some lunch?"

"The kids are probably expecting you home for lunch. You can drop me off at a hotel, and I'll—"

"Nope. I'm going to be a tyrant again, sweetheart. You and I are having lunch. I told Mrs. H. I wouldn't be home to eat. If you refuse me, I'll be destined to eat alone and I hate eating alone."

"Oh, please. You know Mrs. H. would start cooking the moment you walked through the door."

"Not if I came back without you. She ordered me this morning to take care of you."

"She did no such thing."

"Yes, she did, before you came down to the kitchen."

"Rob, you're being ridiculous."

By this time they had reached the Plaza and he parked near a Mexican restaurant. "I feel like Mexican food. How about you? This is a real test of our relationship, by the way. If you don't eat Mexican, it will put a strain on all of us. Even Michael loves nachos."

"Rob—"

He kissed her, briefly and hard. "Please tell me you like nachos."

"Of course I like—"

He kissed her again. "Good. Let's go." He was out of the car, rounding it to her door before she could answer.

After he opened the door for her, she got out and clutched his arm. "Rob, we really shouldn't go to a popular restaurant like this. What if we see someone I know?"

"You're ashamed of me? Now that hurts my feelings."

"Could you possibly be serious for just a minute?" she asked in exasperation.

"Probably not. Come on."

He took her hand and led her across the sidewalk to the restaurant. Since it was after one o'clock, the hostess seated them at once.

After asking Jessica for her preferences, Rob ordered a plate of nachos while they considered the menu. "I'm starved," he warned her.

"After the nachos, I won't be able to eat much else."

"What you can't eat, I'll finish up. It won't go to waste. Or we can take it back home for Mr. H. He loves Mexican food almost as much as I do."

"Doesn't Mrs. Hutchins cook Mexican food?"

"Yeah, but Mr. H. swears it's not as good as this restaurant's." He grinned at Jessica's shocked reaction.

"How can he say that? She's a wonderful cook."

"She'll be glad to know you think so." He shifted his silverware, keeping his gaze on his fingers as he asked, "Do you think— Would you object to having them in your house?"

"Who?"

"Mr. and Mrs. H. I mean, when you marry one day, will you want to manage on your own, or—" He broke off and shifted his gaze to her.

"I won't be able to afford someone like them, but I'm no masochist. If I'm going to continue to work, I suspect I'd enjoy having someone else do the cooking, at least part of the time. And if I ever had children—" She broke off and looked away.

"And?"

"Oh, I was going to say that I can't imagine anyone nicer to help take care of children. Cathy and Michael adore them."

"Yeah. While Sylvia did a good job providing for them, she's, uh, a little self-centered. Mr. and Mrs. H. filled in nicely while I was away."

"You're not thinking of letting them go?" she suddenly asked, a shocked look on her face. "Were you offering to let me hire them? Because I'm not going to have a big place, Rob, and—"

"Of course not. They're part of the family. I was just wondering how someone—maybe for the future—would feel about having someone else run the house."

She looked down at her hands clenched together on the table. "Someone would be very lucky."

He wanted to think she knew he was talking about her, but something about her expression told him she didn't. Either that or she wouldn't be happy to be that someone. He couldn't let himself believe that.

The waitress returned with their drinks and the plate of hot nachos. He watched with pleasure, and a heightened sensuality, as Jessica tasted a nacho and leaned back to moan softly with pleasure.

"I haven't had nachos in ages," she said with a smile.

"Ah, you really do like Mexican food."

"Oh, yes."

He was about to tease her when a man he recognized stopped at their table.

"Does your father know where you are?" Stephen Cattaloni harshly demanded.

Rob gathered himself to enter the fray, not about to let this man browbeat Jessica. But he discovered he didn't need to protect her.

She leaned back against the booth seat and stared coolly at the man. "I doubt it. Does your mistress know where you are?"

Chapter Fourteen

Jessica almost smiled at Stephen's shocked expression.

"Really, Jessica, that's highly inappropriate."

"Is it?"

"I explained to your father—"

"Yes, I heard your explanation. That idea is terribly outdated. By the way, I delivered a retraction of the engagement announcement to the newspaper today."

"Send all the notices you want. But you *will* marry me."

Rob, who had remained quiet until now, leaned forward. "I don't think so."

"Stay out of this," Stephen snapped and then paused to stare at Rob. "Don't I know you from somewhere?"

"No. And I can't stay out of the discussion. Because Jessica is engaged to me."

Fortunately Stephen didn't turn to look at her, because Jessica's mouth fell open. She stared at Rob, wondering why he would make such an announcement. Then she understood. He was rescuing her again.

Rob was a bona fide hero. He'd worked for the FBI until his children needed rescuing. He'd taken her in and then rescued her before her father could find her. Now he was rescuing her again.

For just a moment, she'd thought he loved her. As she loved him. But now she understood. Rescues were his specialty.

Stephen turned back to Jessica and she composed her features. "What's he talking about?"

"You didn't understand what he said?"

"You can't be engaged to him. You're engaged to me."

"Perhaps you should get your ears checked," she said smoothly and picked up her tea glass, as if his presence didn't concern her.

"Listen to me, little girl," the man urged gruffly. "Your father owes me lots of money. You'd better do what he says."

She stared at the man's face, anger in his eyes, and realized her father was willing to sacrifice her to satisfy his own needs. But she wouldn't be a victim.

"If you have money problems with my father, they don't concern me. I'm moving out of his house and I no longer work for him."

"And she's engaged to me," Rob repeated, a smile on his handsome face.

"Who are you?" Stephen demanded, glaring at Rob.

"Rob Berenson."

"That's not—wait a minute, you were with Luciano in Chicago. You're—"

"Undercover FBI."

Stephen froze, then backed away, his hands in the air. "Hey, I'm legit, man. I don't have those connections anymore."

"Wise man," Rob said and saluted him with his tea glass.

"That don't mean I can't cause your father a lot of trouble," he warned, looking at Jessica again.

"I'm sure you can. Dad will have to learn the hard way, I guess." The nonchalance cost her. She had tried so hard to please her father in the past, it wasn't easy to back away now. But she had to.

Stephen growled and spun on his heel to leave the restaurant.

As Jessica sagged against the seat, Rob said, "Now *that* was a bear, Goldilocks. And you did a good job of saving yourself."

"Thanks for helping out, but I think you got a little carried away."

"How? By announcing our engagement? I'm willing to make a sacrifice for you, Goldilocks." His teasing grin made him look more handsome than ever.

"Thanks, but I've decided I'm against sacrifices."

"What's this about not working for your father? You hadn't mentioned that he fired you."

"You wanted to say I told you so?"

His hand stretched across the table and took hold of hers. "No, sweetheart. But it must've hurt."

"I'm luckier than most people who get fired. I've got some money so I can look around for the right new job."

"Jessica, quit pretending being fired was a regular deal. You were fired by your own father."

She stared at their clasped hands, thinking that Rob had given her more support the past few days than her father had in years. "I know. And you're right, it hurts. But only because I've been deluding myself. I've known for a while that he's a selfish man. But he's all the family I have."

"You can become an honorary member of the Berensons, like Mr. and Mrs. H. We'll be your family."

She gave him a faint smile. His offer was generous and sincere. But it wasn't what she wanted. She didn't want to be honorary anything.

"Do you think Stephen was telling the truth? That he's not involved with the mob any longer?" she asked to change the subject.

"I'll make some calls on Monday. If it's true, he's probably trying to buy his way into the upper crust of Kansas City by making your dad the loan and marrying you."

"So there's been no real danger all along?"

"Maybe. Nothing except your father trying to use you for his own ends."

Pain filled her eyes at his reminder and he squeezed her hand. "Hey, let's put such dreary talk out of our heads. Here comes my enchiladas."

ROB KEPT THE CONVERSATION on innocuous topics the rest of their meal. He even managed to elicit a laugh or two from Jessica. But he knew her father's behavior had to have hurt her.

So he planned his next distraction.

"Where are we going?" Jessica asked as they emerged from the restaurant. "The car's back there."

"We have to do a little shopping before we go back home." He held her hand securely in his.

"What kind of shopping?"

"You'll see."

She went along with his plan until he tried to lead her into a famous jewelry store. "Why are we going in here?"

"It's Mrs. H.'s birthday soon. I thought I'd buy her something. You can help me choose." As the wary expression on her face eased slightly, he grabbed a quick kiss and led her through the door.

They wandered around the store, looking at the jewelry displayed there. When Rob indicated a preference for tennis bracelets as a gift for Mrs. Hutchins, he asked Jessica to pick the one she liked best. As she was considering them, he spoke quietly to the salesman.

"This one is the prettiest, but I think it's also the most expensive," she finally said, looking up at him.

"Then that's the one we'll take."

"Here you are, sir," the salesman said as he returned to them, carrying a large black velvet box. "These rings are of the finest quality."

He felt Jessica stiffen beside him and leaned toward her to whisper, "Play along. We want word to get back to Stephen that we're serious."

Her eyes were widened in shock and she blinked several times, as if she hadn't understood what he'd said. "Th-this isn't necessary."

"Just try them on, sweetheart." He pulled her left hand up and laid it on the counter, but she snatched it back. Turning to the salesman, he joked, "She's a little shy."

"These really are exquisite rings. But if you don't like any of them, I can—"

"No! That's not the problem. The rings are gorgeous, but I—I need to talk to my—to Rob for a moment." She tugged on his arm, pulling him away from the counter.

He looked over his shoulder at the salesman, giving him a wink, as if sharing a joke about females. He only hoped he could convince Jessica as easily.

"Rob Berenson, what are you doing?"

"Shopping?"

"Fine. We've found the present for Mrs. Hutchins. Now let's go."

"Look, Jess, I know you're relieved that Cattaloni said he wasn't connected to the mob any longer, but that doesn't mean he's going to give up on forcing you to marry him. The more public you are about being engaged to someone else, the more likely he'll give up."

"Buying an expensive piece of jewelry isn't necessary."

"Hey, I'm not going to keep it. After you wear it a few days, I'll bring it back and tell them you don't like it. Then they'll give me my money back. It's no big deal.''

She blinked several times again, her big blue eyes filling with some emotion he couldn't quite read. Was she upset with his explanation? He wanted to pull her into his arms and assure her he never intended to let her go...or let her take off his ring, but now wasn't the time.

''Pick out the ring you like. It's a smoke screen, okay?'' He pulled her back to the counter. ''She's ready to make a selection now.''

The salesman went into his spiel about the quality of the diamonds. Rob watched Jessica as she looked at the rings. Her eyes lit up at one exquisite setting, a square-cut diamond with a baguette on each side, but she didn't ask to try it on. Instead she selected the smallest of the rings offered.

''Ah, you have great taste, madam. That is the most expensive ring because of the incredible quality of the diamond.''

She immediately returned it to the tray.

Rob waited patiently as she tried on several rings. Her gaze frequently returned to the ring located in the center of the tray, but she never asked to see it.

Finally he picked up the ring and slid it onto her third finger. It was a perfect fit. ''We'll take this one.''

''Rob, you can't—''

''This one,'' he said firmly. ''And she'll wear it.''

Jessica was staring at the ring. When she realized he was watching her, she moved to take it off.

He covered her hand with his. ''Leave it on.''

The salesman accepted his credit card and left with the other diamonds.

"Rob, are you sure they'll give you your money back?"

He kissed her, briefly, though his hunger demanded more, and smiled at her. "They're very accommodating here."

That was a general enough response. He didn't want Jessica to know, at this point, that he had no intention of returning the ring.

JESSICA STARED at her ring—*the* ring—amazed that it was on her finger. She'd liked it best at once, but she didn't know how Rob had figured that out. It was going to be torture when she had to return it. She found the fantasy of an engagement to Rob too attractive as it was, without wearing the ring.

"Where are we going now?"

"Home. We need to pick up Mrs. H. to help us."

"Help us what?"

"Go pack your belongings."

She'd been about to remove the ring, but his words stopped her. "What are you talking about?"

"I heard you ask your father to have the housekeeper start packing your belongings. But I doubt that he gave the order. So I figured Mrs. H. could help us."

"Rob, I don't have anywhere to put everything yet. I need to wait until I find an apartment. I—I don't have a home." She swallowed the rising panic.

"Sure you do, sweetheart. With us. I told you we were making you a part of our family."

"Rob, I appreciate you rescuing me, really I do. But enough is enough." He was getting carried away with his role of knight in shining armor. It was a good thing she wasn't trying to take advantage of him, or she'd have a great lawsuit when he took back the ring.

"Okay, how about this? You can get your things out of your father's house and store them with us until you find a place to live. You don't want to make a rash decision."

"I think a rash decision is exactly what is called for. I need to find a place to live and a job at once."

"I think I've lined up a job for you."

She stared at him, her thoughts all jumbled. "What are you talking about? You didn't even know Dad fired me until we were having lunch. I've been with you every minute since then. How could you find me a job? And what business is it of yours where I work?"

"You're getting testy, now. I'm just trying to help."

"I think you're trying to take over my life. I'm quite capable of finding a job. I'm a good accountant."

"I'm counting on it. How could I recommend you if I didn't think you were the best?" He gave her a boyish grin.

"Rob!" she protested in exasperation. "This isn't— Oh! We're here!" She started tugging at the ring on her finger.

"What are you doing?"

"I can't wear the ring here. The kids would think that we were— I mean—"

"Going to marry?"

"Yes. And I won't be a party to misleading Cathy and Michael." She was going to suffer enough heartbreak. There was no point in spreading it around.

After he parked the car, he studied her. "Okay," he finally agreed with a nod. "Take it off while we're here, but put it back on before we go to your father's. It will help convince him."

"I haven't agreed to go to my father's!"

He grinned as he opened his door. "I know, but I'm going to convince you."

WHICH, OF COURSE, he did.

Jessica reminded herself that she needed to take charge of her life. But she also didn't want to fight him about something she wanted. It seemed important now that she completely break her ties to her father.

Not that she would refuse to see him or talk to him, if he needed her, but she no longer intended to follow her father's orders.

So, she accepted Mrs. Hutchins's willing assistance and the three of them headed to her home, leaving the children with Mr. Hutchins.

Once they were in the car, Rob ordered, "Put the ring back on."

She glanced nervously over her shoulder at Mrs. Hutchins sitting in the back seat. "Uh, Rob thought it would help if we pretended to be engaged, Mrs. Hutchins. He bought a ring, but he's going to return it afterward.''

"Oh? Let me see. I love diamonds.''

Rob grinned. "Why didn't I think of that? I've already bought your birthday present, Mrs. H.''

"Quit your teasing, Rob. My, that's a beautiful ring.''

"I didn't want to wear it in front of Michael and Cathy because they wouldn't have understood.''

Jessica watched uneasily as the other two exchanged a look in the rearview mirror. What was Rob saying silently to his housekeeper?

"That's real thoughtful of you, dear.''

"We probably won't pack everything of Jessica's,'' Rob said, changing the subject. "But her personal items, clothes, etc., should be moved today.''

"Rob, I just need enough for a few days, until I find a place to stay. Remember?'' She'd told him several times she wasn't moving in with him and his family. But it was like talking to a stone wall.

They pulled into the long circular driveway in front of her house. The thought of another confrontation with her father distressed her, but it couldn't be avoided.

Rob must've sensed her mood because he came around the car and lifted her left hand to his lips, kissing it beside the ring. "Everything will be all right.''

She rang the doorbell and then used her key to unlock the door. "I don't want to sneak in. I haven't done anything wrong.''

"Of course you haven't," Mrs. Hutchins agreed, her placid smile reassuring Jessica.

"Jessica!" the housekeeper, Mrs. Anders, exclaimed as she saw them enter. "You're back. Your father has been so worried."

"Yes, I'm back. We're going upstairs to pack a few of my things. We won't be here long."

"Pack your things? Are you going away again?" the housekeeper asked in surprise.

"My father didn't ask you to pack for me?" She avoided the knowing look in Rob's eyes. He'd been right about her father's behavior.

"Why, no. He didn't tell me you were taking a trip."

Jessica squared her shoulders and said calmly, "I'm not. I'm moving out. We'll pack as much as we can and then I'll let you know later where to send everything."

She led the way up the curving staircase, seeing her home with a new eye. While it wasn't as formal as Rob's ex's house, it wasn't as warm as she'd thought. Maybe she was remembering the house as it was when her mother was alive.

"I'm glad your father decided not to sell, sweetheart. I don't think the house would suit us. Do you, Mrs. H.?" Rob asked, looking at his housekeeper.

"It's a nice house, but a bit oversized, don't you think?" She huffed a little as she continued up the stairs. "I think you could go days without seeing anyone, if you wanted."

Her words struck Jessica because she *had* gone days without seeing her father. If she had a family, she'd want them closer together. "Yes, you can," she agreed.

When they reached her suite of rooms, Rob walked to the window seat at once. "Well, we may not buy this house, but we're going to have to find Cathy a window seat. She'd love this."

"I didn't mean to cause problems," Jessica apologized.

"Cause problems?" he repeated with a teasing grin. "That's all you've done since we met you, Goldilocks."

"Rob Berenson, how can you say such a thing to this sweet girl?" Mrs. Hutchins protested.

Jessica wasn't sure he was teasing. She knew she'd disrupted their lives. But Rob crossed the room and drew her into his embrace.

"Check out the other room, Mrs. H., while I reassure Jessica I was teasing."

"No—" She never finished her protest because Rob didn't wait for his housekeeper's departure before kissing Jessica. Unlike the brief kisses he'd given her at various times during the day, this kiss was completely consuming, and her arms went around his neck as she pressed against him. This kiss was a reminder of what they'd shared last night. This kiss made her heart sing.

Until Mrs. Hutchins interrupted them. Which was just as well since Jessica had been fighting the urge to tear Rob's clothes off.

"That's enough of that, Rob. We've got some packing to do. I found some suitcases in the back of your closet, Jessica. Should I start with the chest or the clothes hanging in the closet?''

Jessica tried to pull her thoughts together. "Um, the chest, please. I'll start with the closet.''

"Jessica?'' her father's housekeeper said from the door, making Jessica glad she'd pulled herself from Rob's embrace. "I found some packing boxes you might want to use.''

"Thank you, Mrs. Anders. That's very helpful of you,'' Jessica said in surprise. She hadn't expected any assistance from her father's staff.

"Your father does know you're moving out?'' the woman asked anxiously.

"Yes, of course. I told him myself.'' She watched the relief on the woman's face. She knew anyone who'd crossed her father once would prefer not to do so again.

"Shall I help pack?''

"If you don't mind and won't be neglecting your other duties, we'd appreciate the help.''

As the woman moved into the bedroom, Rob saluted Jessica and asked, "What are my duties, general?''

"If you're trying to comment on my bossiness, that's a case of the pot calling the kettle black, Rob Berenson.''

"I was showing respect for your command of the situation,'' he told her with a wide-eyed innocence that didn't fool her.

"If you really want to help—''

"I get to pack your underwear?'' His leering stare was comical, as he'd intended, she supposed.

"No! But if you'll look in that closet, I'd like you to pick out a stuffed animal each for Michael and Cathy. I'm going to have Mrs. Anders give the rest of them to charities."

With another salute that had her shaking her head at his clowning, he disappeared into the big closet.

Jessica stood there, her hands clasped together, trying to adjust to the changes in her life. Somehow, saying she was moving out of her home and actually doing it were two different things.

Suddenly someone grabbed her left hand and held it up. "I'm glad you've finally come to your senses!" her father snapped.

Chapter Fifteen

Rob had only heard that harsh male voice once before, on the phone, but he recognized it.

He moved to the door of the closet. The man, who didn't resemble Jessica at all, held her left hand up in the air.

"Hello, Dad," Jessica said calmly.

Rob was proud of how well she handled these stressful moments. But it seemed too much for her to have to face down Stephen and her father in one day. And it was all Rob's fault.

"Hello, Mr. Barnes," he said, stepping forward. "I'm glad you approve."

"Who are you?"

"I'm the man who put that ring on your daughter's finger."

"Don't be ridiculous! My daughter is engaged to Stephen Cattaloni."

"No, she's—"

"*Excuse* me!" Jessica interrupted. "I am not a ghost. Quit talking as if I weren't here."

Rob grinned and ducked his head for a brief kiss before responding. "Yes, ma'am."

"Who is this man?" her father demanded.

"Rob Berenson."

"Did you accept this ring from him?"

Rob didn't attempt to answer for her, waiting as her gaze met his.

"Yes, I did."

"What about Stephen?"

Jessica pulled her hand from her father's grip. "I believe I've already told you I didn't intend to marry Stephen. And I've told Stephen the same thing."

"He didn't believe you. I explained that you were jealous." Her father continued to glare at her, and Rob fought the urge to punch him out.

"I've talked to Stephen since last night, Dad. He knows I have no intention of marrying him. In fact, he met Rob."

"You can't do this to me! I'm your father."

Rob started to speak. He had the greatest urge to inform this man of the meaning of fatherhood. He'd learned a lot about it the past couple of weeks. But Jessica shook her head at him.

"I don't believe I'm doing anything to you, Dad. You told me Stephen loaned you the money out of friendship."

Harshly the man threw out his hand, as if erasing his words. "He loaned me the money because he wanted you to establish him in good society."

"You've never mentioned that concept before."

Jessica's voice was smooth, calm, but Rob noticed her fingers trembling. He moved over to hold her hand.

"You're not a child, Jessica. Arranged marriages

are made all the time,'' her father assured her with a superior air.

"Hopefully the participants of those marriages aren't lied to about them." She turned to Rob then, and he realized she'd about reached her limit.

"Go help Mrs. H. finish up, and we'll get out of here," he whispered.

As her father prepared to follow her, obviously still intending to try to run roughshod over her, Rob moved to block his path. "Mr. Barnes, Jessica is picking up some of her things. We'll let you know where to send the rest of her belongings later."

"I'll send nothing. I own everything in this house!"

"Oh? It was my understanding that Jessica owns half of everything."

The man's face turned red with anger, making his blond-and-gray hair appear even paler. "I don't know who you are, but don't think you're getting a thing out of me. I won't be milked for my money."

"I wouldn't dream of it. But you will surrender everything that is Jessica's, or she'll see you in court."

"So, you're marrying her for her money? I always warned her about that. I thought you had better sense!" he exclaimed, staring over Rob's shoulder.

Rob turned around, wondering if Jessica would believe her father's words. She smiled grimly at John Barnes. "Is it any better for my father to sell me for a million dollars? You've done exactly what you warned me about. I didn't know you were talking about yourself."

As her father gaped at her, Jessica looked at Rob. "We're ready. Can you help us with the luggage?"

"Sure." He met Mrs. H. at the door with two suitcases. "Are there more?"

"Yes, Robbie. There are three more. If you could get the two big ones—"

"Here, Mrs. Hutchins, I'll take those," Jessica said, reaching for the suitcases the older woman was carrying. "If you'll get the small one on the bed, we'll leave now."

Rob followed Jessica from the bedroom, weighted down by two large suitcases. Mrs. Hutchins picked up the small one and preceded them from the sitting room, followed by Mrs. Anders. John Barnes remained standing in the middle of the room.

"I'm not going to let you leave, Jessica," he threatened, blocking her path.

This time Rob didn't wait for Jessica to fight her own battle. He set down the luggage and stepped in front of her. "If you want a fight, I'll be glad to oblige. I don't like the way you've treated your own daughter, and I think you deserve a black eye. Interested?"

"Don't be absurd. I'm not going to fight you."

"Then you're not going to stop Jessica from leaving."

"I'm her family!" John snapped.

"No, Dad," Jessica replied quietly behind Rob. "Family are people who care about you. You only care about yourself."

"I raised you, young lady! I provided you with all the fancy clothes you're carrying out of here, with a private school education, with all those vacations!''

"No, Dad. Granddad's money, my mother's money, provided all of that. In the thirty years since you married Mother, you've managed to lose a fortune.''

"You needn't think you'll see any more money from me!'' he rapidly replied, his face turning red again.

"No, I doubt I will.'' With those words, she stepped around him and continued on.

"How dare she!'' When the man realized his only audience was Rob, who'd promised to blacken his eye, he backed up several steps.

"She has no right to speak to me like that.''

Rob grinned, proud of Jessica. "My lawyer will contact you on Jessica's behalf to settle the money issue. Probably she'll refuse to prosecute if mismanagement of her money is found—'' he thought his adversary was going to pass out, his cheeks went so pale "—but we'll see.''

Maybe his parting shot was better than blackening the man's eye, but it wasn't as satisfactory. But Rob grinned as he followed Jessica and Mrs. H. out of the house. At least he'd been able to deliver some kind of blow.

JESSICA COLLAPSED against the car seat, drained from the trauma of the past few minutes.

"Are you okay, dear?'' Mrs. Hutchins asked softly.

"Yes, of course. It was…difficult.''

She was relieved when Rob joined them. "You didn't— I mean, he's lots older than you are."

"No, I didn't hit him, sweetheart. But I wanted to. He's a selfish bastard."

"Robbie! Mind your manners," Mrs. Hutchins warned from the back seat.

He grinned at her. "It may be bad manners to say so, Mrs. H., but you know I'm right."

Jessica covered her face with her hands, her shoulders shaking. She couldn't stand much more.

"Shh, baby, don't cry," Rob urged, pulling her against him. "I didn't mean to hurt you."

She allowed herself the luxury of leaning against him for a few seconds. Then she shook her head and sat back in her seat. "Sorry. Can we go?"

"You bet." He pulled through the driveway and had them on their way.

She worried her bottom lip with her teeth. "You can drop me at one of the hotels near the Plaza, if you would."

"Nope. You're coming home with us."

"Rob, I have to take care of myself."

"You will. But not tonight. I'll take you to a hotel tomorrow night, if you want." He looked at her and then turned his attention back to his driving. "Besides, you haven't told Cathy and Michael goodbye yet."

She sagged back against the seat, unable to fight him right now. And she hadn't said goodbye to the children. But she couldn't think of them now. The enormity of what she'd just done began to sink in.

"I'm starting completely over," she muttered.

Rob reached over and caught her clasped hands. "How convenient. So am I. We can combine forces and take the world by storm."

She tried a smile, but she wasn't sure she pulled it off.

AFTER ANOTHER NIGHT spent at Rob's house, Jessica rose full of determination. She was starting all over again, but she would make it. She'd find a place to live, another job, another life. In truth, she realized she regretted little she'd left behind.

Since her mother's death, her world had never been happy or secure. She'd chased her father's affection, not realizing he had none to bestow. Now she was free to pursue her own dreams.

Too bad they were unattainable.

More than all the wealth in the world, she wanted family. She wanted warmth. She wanted love.

She stared at the ring on her finger. Last night, she'd convinced herself the ring would be safer on her hand than in a box in the drawer. After coming to bed, she'd put it on and dreamed of a future where she'd never remove it.

Family, warmth and love abounded in the Berenson family. Cathy and Michael had helped last night, offering her hugs and an invitation to stay with them forever once Rob had explained that she had no home. Mr. and Mrs. Hutchins had accepted her presence in the house as normal.

Rob, however, had kept his distance. There had been very little touching, no kissing and no attempt to get her alone. Didn't he even want her anymore?

For all his offers of a home, he'd never mentioned anything permanent. He'd rescued her more than once in the past few days, but she wanted so much more. She'd fallen in love with the bossy, gentle, teasing man.

It amazed her that her perception of love and marriage could change so quickly. In the past, she'd pictured a calm, stately marriage, each participant moving to his own schedule. Marriage to Rob, and his kids, would be messy, chaotic, intense…and wonderful.

But even if she could bring herself to marry someone who might think she was after *his* money, it appeared Rob didn't want her that way. He would rescue her, even become temporarily engaged to her, but he didn't want her.

She dressed and carefully repacked what little she'd disturbed in her suitcases before going downstairs. It was time for her to move on, to become responsible for herself. Maybe, if she was lucky, she could see Cathy and Michael occasionally.

"Good morning," she said as she entered the kitchen. Only the Hutchinses were there.

"Good morning," Mrs. Hutchins replied and rose at once. "I saved breakfast for you. Are you feeling all right?"

"I'm fine. I didn't go to sleep until late last night, so I'm afraid I overslept."

Mr. Hutchins smiled at her. "Amazing you could do that with those two young'uns racing around this morning."

"Where are they?"

"The three of them went to early church," Mrs. Hutchins explained as she carried food to the table. She chuckled and added, "Those two kids wouldn't go until their daddy promised you'd still be here when they got back."

Jessica nodded. "Of course I'll be here. It would be impolite to leave without saying goodbye after all they've done for me. But I'll move to a hotel this afternoon."

"We have plenty of room," Mr. Hutchins said before turning his attention back to the Sunday paper.

Mrs. Hutchins began making luncheon preparations and Jessica shared the paper with Mr. Hutchins, relaxing in the peaceful quiet of a Sunday morning.

Half an hour later, the sound of a car in the driveway announced the return of Rob and the children. In spite of her warnings to herself, Jessica couldn't help the anticipation that rose in her. She told herself it was because she missed the children.

Her heart knew it was because she'd missed Rob.

"Jessica!" Cathy exclaimed as she rushed through the door directly into Jessica's outstretched arms. Michael was right behind his sister and demanded a greeting, too.

To Jessica's surprise, based on his behavior last night, Rob kissed her on her forehead as his children hugged her.

"Did you get some rest?" he asked, grinning.

"Yes, thank you for letting me sleep. I apologize for being such a rude guest. I'll go to a hotel this—"

"Good," he replied, ignoring what she was saying, "because we've got a big day planned."

"What?"

"We're going out for lunch and then the Realtor has several houses to show us. Plus, a friend called who has a chocolate Labrador retriever who's had puppies. We're going to pick out Cathy and Michael's puppies. And they insist you help them."

"Rob, I can't stay with you forever. I need to go to a hotel."

"I'll take you after we get home."

She blinked several times at his ready agreement. It only confirmed what she'd already suspected. He was happy to rescue her, but he wasn't planning a future that included her.

"Thank you. I'd love to see the puppies."

Cathy, still standing beside her, said, "We have to think up good names, too. I've never named a dog before."

"Me, neither, sweetie, but I'm sure you'll do a great job."

"Why do you have to go away?" Cathy asked, leaning closer.

Jessica hugged her. "Because I'm all grown up. I'm supposed to take care of myself."

"Will you ever come see us?"

"Of course I will. And if you buy one of the houses you look at today, I'll even know where to find you." She cuddled Cathy a little closer, dreading the moment to come when they'd be separated.

"Are you ready to go?" Rob asked, and she looked up to find his gaze on her and his daughter.

"Yes, I suppose. Should I change?" She was wearing the bright blue pantsuit she'd bought during their shopping expedition.

"You look perfect to me," he told her with a smile that warmed her to her toes.

Before she could hope his smile had any significance, he turned to the Hutchinses. "You two need to come, too, to be sure you like whatever we might want to buy. After all, it'll be your home, too."

"But I was going to fix fried chicken for lunch," Mrs. Hutchins protested.

"Nope, the whole family's going out to lunch. You deserve a day off from the stove," Rob assured Mrs. Hutchins, giving her a kiss on the cheek. A kiss as friendly as the one he'd given Jessica earlier.

Within a few minutes, they all headed for the car. To Jessica's surprise, Rob asked Mr. Hutchins to drive and insisted Mrs. Hutchins ride in the seat beside him.

Then he put his two children in one seat belt in the back seat, Jessica in the center, and him by the other window.

"Hope you're not too crowded," he said as he closed the car door. "Here, this will help." He put his arm behind her.

Spacewise, his action was beneficial, giving her a little more room. But that room left her almost in his embrace, tucked under his arm, her head very easily resting on him. She tried to sit upright, to avoid as much contact as possible, but she couldn't keep her body rigid for long.

As she finally relaxed against him, his hand

curved around her shoulder. "That's good. I was afraid you'd remain as stiff as a poker all day."

"I didn't want to impose on you," she muttered, not looking at him.

"Impose all you want," he assured her. "I kind of like it."

"Daddy, does this house have a window seat?" Cathy interrupted, stretching up to see out the window.

"I'm not sure, but if we like the rest of the house, we might be able to add a window seat." He bent down and murmured into Jessica's ear. "See what you started?"

She turned to look at him, sure he was teasing. At once his lips covered hers in a brief kiss.

"Daddy, it's not good-night," Michael said.

The other three, the Hutchinses and Cathy, stared at Michael and Rob, confused.

"Child, what are you talking about?" Mrs. Hutchins asked Michael.

"Daddy was kissing Jessica good-night but the sun is shining."

Jessica felt her cheeks burn but she said nothing. It was up to Rob to explain his behavior.

"I forgot to kiss her good-night last night, son, so I was just catching up," he explained, with a casual tone that instantly reassured the little boy.

"Oh. Look, there's a dog!"

The animal successfully distracted Michael, but Mrs. Hutchins gave Jessica an approving smile and Cathy looked at her with interest. Jessica ducked her head.

ROB ENJOYED LUNCH with his family. But he'd rather have had Jessica alone. His hunger for her was growing faster than he could handle. Last night, with more time spent in his house, with his children, he'd backed away from touching Jessica, afraid he'd give in to his desire for her.

That's why he was ready to take her to a hotel tonight. There would be no prying eyes or ears, no children to shelter. Tonight, the two of them would be alone.

Until then, he needed to concentrate on finding a house. He wanted everything settled as soon as possible. As hard as it was, he tried not to think about making love to Jessica. Not yet.

The first house was too stiff and formal, not a happy place. The second house was not in good condition. It would've taken a lot of work before they could move in.

When they pulled up in front of the third house, in Mission Hills, the exclusive neighborhood on the Kansas side of the city where Sylvia's house was located, everyone gave an anticipatory sigh. It was a beautiful home, two-story, stately without being stodgy. There were lots of trees around it and a creek flowed nearby.

"I like this one, Daddy," Michael announced.

The real estate salesman led them into the house, and they were all in agreement with Michael. The rooms were spacious, with lots of windows. There were plenty of bedrooms, with a downstairs suite for the Hutchinses, almost like a private apartment.

Mrs. Hutchins enthused over the kitchen, a huge

room with all the latest equipment, while Mr. Hutchins found a workroom in the garage to his taste. The children immediately began choosing their own rooms, and Cathy was ecstatic when she found a window seat overlooking the backyard and the creek.

Rob took Jessica's hand and continued down the hall until he reached the master bedroom. The two of them paused on the doorstep, and Jessica sighed contentedly.

"You like it?"

"What's not to like? The fireplace is beautiful with plenty of space for a conversation area. It has huge windows. I want to see the bath," she added and headed in the direction of the door at one end of the room.

Opening it, she stopped again. "Oh, Rob," she muttered, waiting for him to join her. "It has a sunken tub with jet streams."

As he reached her side, she continued on to look at the closets. "Huge closets. It's perfect. Look, there's two closets. How incredible!"

"Ah, I gather closets are important in your opinion," he teased.

"Oh, yes. Every woman—" She stopped abruptly and he waited for her to continue. "I'm sure you'll enjoy them."

"Do you like the house?"

"It's a lovely house, but my opinion doesn't matter. Mr. and Mrs. Hutchins and the children are the ones you should be asking."

Rob raised his eyebrows and grinned at her. He

didn't need to ask anyone. He knew they'd found their house. Now all he had to do was convince Jessica that she was a part of their family. And belonged right here in this bedroom, in this bed, with him. The thought sent shafts of pleasure coursing through his body.

Chapter Sixteen

Choosing the puppies was even easier than choosing a house.

After Rob had a private discussion with the real estate salesman, they drove south from the city to his friend's house. Charles, Rob's friend, led them all to his backyard where the mother of the puppies was holding court. The puppies had only opened their eyes a few days ago and it would be several weeks before they could leave their mother.

"Perfect," Rob announced. "We should be in the house about then."

"The house we saw today?" Cathy asked eagerly.

"We've made an offer, so we should hear today or tomorrow, baby."

Jessica held her breath, afraid to breathe, knowing it would hurt to think of the others in that beautiful home, where she wanted to be. However, Cathy distracted her, tugging on her hand.

"Jessica, which puppy should I choose?"

They both knelt down beside the roly-poly puppies. "Oh, Cathy, they're all adorable."

"I want this one," Michael announced, pointing

to an adventuresome puppy, straying from the other five.

"Would you like to pick him up?" Charles offered.

Michael looked both eager and frightened. "Will it hurt him?"

"Not at all." Charles scooped up the puppy Michael had chosen and placed it in his hands. "Just be gentle and don't drop him."

"Me, too. Can I hold one?" Cathy pleaded, excitement in her voice.

"Maybe you should both sit down on the ground," Rob suggested. "It would be a long fall for the puppies if they slipped out of your hands."

Michael plopped down at once, his gaze never leaving the small animal.

Jessica sat down, too, and Cathy crawled in her lap. "Will you help me?" she asked in a whisper.

"Sure. Which puppy do you like?"

"The littlest one."

Charles frowned. "That's the runt of the litter, Cathy. It may not be the strongest."

"I'll take good care of it, I promise. Jessica, you'll help me, won't you?"

Jessica swallowed, her throat suddenly dry. How could she promise that when she wouldn't be around. "I—"

"Of course she will," Rob interrupted, smiling at her.

Charles placed the puppy in Cathy's lap. She and Jessica both stroked the wriggly warm body, and a tiny pink tongue appeared, licking both their hands.

"Look!" Cathy squealed. "It likes us."

Jessica hugged Cathy. "Of course he, uh, it does." She looked at Charles. "Is this one a boy or a girl?"

"Female. Michael's is male."

"Are they all going to stay dark?" Rob asked.

"I doubt it. The father is a golden Lab. The little one Cathy likes is already showing a lighter coat."

Cathy listened intently, then a huge smile burst across her face. "I know the name for my puppy. I'm going to name her after you, Jessica."

They all stared at her. "You're going to name your puppy Jessica?" Rob finally asked.

"No, of course not! I'm going to name her Goldilocks!"

While Charles and the Hutchinses still looked confused, Rob, Jessica and his children burst into laughter.

"And I'm going to name mine Bear," Michael added, still laughing. "But we need two more, Daddy."

"No, I don't think so. This family is growing fast enough as it is. We'll stick with two dogs today."

WHEN THEY RETURNED HOME, Mrs. Hutchins began frying the chicken she'd planned for lunch earlier. Jessica reminded Rob about taking her to a hotel, but he asked her to postpone her departure until after they'd eaten. He left her in the kitchen with the children clamoring for her to stay.

When he returned a few minutes later, it was to

announce that the seller had accepted their offer on the house.

Everyone cheered.

"Does that mean we can move there tomorrow?" Michael asked.

"Nope, it'll take a week or two, Michael," Rob assured him. "Just a week or two and we can start our new life together." He smiled at Jessica.

She turned away and began helping Mrs. Hutchins with the meal. After all, she wasn't going to be a part of their new life.

After dinner, Rob asked if she'd mind waiting until the children went to bed. He'd called and made her a reservation at a hotel nearby, and they'd hold the room late.

Of course, she agreed. After all, it would've been rude to demand that he take her at once. Besides, saying good-night and goodbye to the children was important.

After tucking Michael in and kissing him goodbye, Jessica and Rob entered Cathy's room. She didn't look the least bit sleepy, but Jessica kissed her and promised to visit in their new house.

"I have a question, Daddy," Cathy announced.

"What's that, baby?"

"Michael and I have two daddies now, don't we?"

Rob raised his eyebrows. "I guess you do, though I'm the best daddy, aren't I?" He grinned and tickled his daughter.

"Of course. But if we have two daddies, why can't we have two mommies?"

Jessica felt the blood drain from her cheeks. She didn't want to hear Rob's answer. "I'd better go finish packing while your father explains, uh, everything to you, sweetheart. Bye-bye."

She scooted out of the room before either of them could stop her. But they didn't try.

In the room she'd used, she closed the last suitcase and sat down on the edge of the bed, waiting for Rob. So much had happened in the last few days. Her life had irrevocably changed.

Not that she would return to her pre-Rob days. But the swirl of emotions made decisions difficult. The only clear need had been a gravitation to the warmth and love she'd found in this family. It reminded her of her life before her mother's death.

Maybe she wasn't really in love with Rob. Maybe it was his family she coveted. Maybe she wasn't attracted to him.

She laughed out loud at such foolishness. Not attracted to him. The other night she'd been willing to make love to him in the kitchen, for heaven's sake! Even if she took away Cathy, Michael, the Hutchinses, she'd still want to spend her life with Rob.

But she didn't want him to pursue her because he thought she needed rescuing, or because his children wanted her as a mother.

"Ready?" Rob asked from the doorway, and she jumped in embarrassment.

She certainly hoped he couldn't read her thoughts.

"Yes, of course. Shall we ask Mr. Hutchins to help with the bags, or make two trips?"

"There's no need to take all of that now. Just take a bag for a couple of days. You can store the rest here until you decide where you're going to live."

"Are you sure? I don't want to be a bother."

"Jess, the room is empty. How can it hurt to store your bags here?" He moved into the room. "Which bag do you want to take?"

She pointed out a large bag and picked up the overnight case that contained her makeup and nightgown.

"Ha! You would pick the largest," he complained, but he was grinning. His humor was the nicest thing about Rob. Well, one of the nicest, she amended, watching his muscles bulge as he lifted the case.

Downstairs, she thanked the Hutchinses for their kindness and then Rob whisked her out to the car.

"If we stayed much longer, Mrs. H. was going to start crying and beg you to stay."

Clearly that wasn't what Rob wanted. She bit her bottom lip.

"She's been very kind to me."

"She wasn't that happy with Sylvia. Mr. H. says her disposition has improved a lot since Sylvia left."

Jessica was surprised. She couldn't imagine the grandmotherly Mrs. Hutchins being anything less than warm. "He's probably just teasing."

Rob chuckled. "Sylvia is bossy and unappreciative. I doubt that he is."

Jessica wasn't going to defend the absent Sylvia, especially when she hadn't heard anything she could admire about her, so they drove to the hotel in silence.

When they reached the hotel, Rob had a bellboy take her bags and escorted her to the counter. "I'll be glad to take care of the check-in," he assured her.

"No. You've rescued me enough. I have to take care of myself, thank you." She'd decided standing on her own two feet was the way to convince Rob that she had something to offer him.

He stood back as she signed in and offered her credit card. Afterward, she turned and held out her hand. "I want to thank you for all your help, Rob. Oh! I need to give you back my—the ring. It's in my luggage."

"I'll come upstairs with you," he said, taking her arm and leading her to the elevators. The bellboy followed with her bags on a rolling cart.

She noticed a small duffel bag with her things. "That's not my bag," she said, pointing it out.

"He knows," Rob said, nodding at the bellboy. He pushed the elevator button and the door of the one nearest them opened.

Her room was on the seventh floor. Within minutes, they were standing in the center of the elegant room. "If you'll put the suitcase on the bed, I'd appreciate it," Jessica ordered and opened her purse for a tip.

Rob pulled some bills from his pocket and handed them to the bellboy before he could follow her orders. "I've got it," he told him. "Thanks for your help."

Jessica was distracted by his helping her again. "I could've given him a tip, Rob. You've got to stop rescuing me. I'm really quite capable—oh, no! He forgot the other bag." She moved toward the phone. "I'll call him back."

"UH, JESSICA, he didn't make a mistake." Rob swallowed before he continued. The bag was going to be a little awkward to explain. "You see, that's my bag."

She spun around to stare at him. "Why would you—"

Her eyes grew larger and she stared from the bag to him and back to the bag.

He hurriedly tried to explain. "It's not what you think. I mean, it is, but the decision is yours. But—hell, Jess, the other night in the kitchen, we both wanted—I can't make love to you at home right now, with the kids next door, liable to walk in on us any minute."

The appalled look on her face wasn't encouraging. He cleared his throat and tried again. "Jess, I—"

"You've helped me a lot in the past few days, and I'll be glad to pay you, Rob, but I don't pay with my body." Her words had gotten colder and more stilted until the final one was like an ice cube.

"I didn't mean that, Jessica!" he roared, stunned that she would interpret his behavior as a request for payment. "How could you think that?"

"Very easily. You waltz into my hotel room with

an overnight bag and announce you're staying. We haven't—''

"No, we haven't! And I'm tired of going to bed frustrated! I want—''

"You've made your wants quite clear!''

"Jessica, I'm trying—''

"Obviously!'' she drawled with anger. "I suppose you're better than Stephen because your action says you're attracted to me, but it's not much better.''

"Attracted to you? Do you really think what I feel for you can be described so innocuously when it's eating me up inside? I've been a gentleman when what I wanted to be was a caveman!''

He saw a flicker of emotion in her eyes that gave him hope, but it died as she spoke. "I think you'd better go now.''

"All right. Fine. I'll go. But I think I deserve a good-night kiss before I do.'' He didn't give her time to agree, because he suspected what her answer would be.

Pulling her against him, he covered her lips with his. His hands roamed her body, framing it, coaxing it, while his mouth devoured her. By the time he finally released her, his breathing was labored and every ounce of his body was craving more Jessica.

"We'll talk tomorrow, when you're rational!'' he snapped, frustration lacing his words.

He regretted his harshness when he saw tears in her big blue eyes. To his surprise, she reached out to clasp his collar.

"No. Don't go. I want this as much as you.''

With a sigh, she sagged against him, her mouth meeting his.

His conscience nagged him, warning him something was wrong. His body overruled his head. For all the times he'd resisted the temptation she represented, his body urged completion, satisfaction. Heaven.

"Sweetheart, you're sure?" he did manage to mutter after coming up for air.

She didn't bother with words, her lips surging against his, inviting, tempting him until he could think no longer.

Their clothes came off faster than they had in the kitchen. He stroked her curves, learning every inch of her body. As she did the same, he discovered an awakening in him he'd never felt before. A sense of belonging, of rightness, he'd never experienced.

As they joined together, Rob was filled with a surreal pleasure to end all pleasures. Jessica was his and he was hers, together, united for all time.

HE WAS GONE.

Jessica raised her head and stared tragically at the indentation on the pillow beside her.

What had she done?

With a sob that refused to be stifled, she buried her head in her pillow.

"You idiot!" she finally muttered. "How could you have expected anything else? All he ever said was that he wanted you."

As she'd wanted him.

But she wanted so much more. Cathy, Michael,

even the Hutchinses. A home filled with warmth and caring. And most of all, a husband who would love her forever.

Instead she'd settled for a one-night fling.

With a sigh, she threw back the covers and got up, wincing slightly at the unaccustomed stiffness. Though talking had been scarce through the night, lovemaking hadn't. She was shocked at the hunger Rob awakened in her, and she took her pleasure from his body like a starving woman. Even now, with the pain of his disappearance, she felt filled from his lovemaking.

As she stood under a stream of hot water, Jessica wondered what her next move should be. In spite of the disappointment that he had left her without even awakening her, she wasn't going to give up. She'd fight for her dreams.

If nothing else, his behavior last night had proven he was attracted to her. But how could she convince him to love her?

She stepped out of the shower with no answers. Wrapping a towel around her, she opened the door to the bedroom where her clothes were waiting.

What should she do now?

She wasn't going to run anymore. That was the one decision she could make. With or without Rob and his family, she was going to get on with her life.

Today she'd see the family attorney, sort out her legal affairs. Her father wasn't financially intelligent. After losing so much money all the years he was married to her mother, he shouldn't have control of any of Jessica's assets.

Then, when she had established herself, found another job, gotten on with her life, she would contact her father again. Perhaps, now that she'd grown up, she could establish some kind of relationship with him.

After all, he was all the family she had.

"ALL RIGHT, SIMS, that should wrap everything up. I'm glad Cattaloni agreed to cut his losses." Rob sat back in his chair and let out the breath he didn't know he was holding. He couldn't wait now to go upstairs and tell Jess the great news. He'd cut out of their room quietly early that morning and arranged for a small private meeting room in the hotel where he could contact Sims and set things straight with one Stephen Cattaloni. He'd known Sims would never deny him help.

"That doesn't mean your girlfriend's father won't have to repay the loan, you know." Sims cut into his thoughts. "We can't do anything about that arrangement, since it's legit. But thankfully we found a couple of other things Cattaloni was up to that provided some encouragement for him to relocate."

"Yeah. And the Bahamas are a long way from Kansas City." Rob hoped Jessica would be pleased. Now she wouldn't have to worry about bumping into the guy. Rob wanted to insure that she'd be happy in Kansas City. With him.

"You haven't changed your mind about coming back to us, have you, Rob? We need you."

Rob chuckled. "Nope. And the last time you tried to persuade me, you made my girlfriend think I was in the mob. So no more calls like those."

To his credit Sims didn't try to persuade him anymore. "But what are you going to do with yourself? I know you. Just having money won't be enough to satisfy you."

"You're right. I'm going to start my own security firm. Try to cut down on the white-collar element. Maybe reduce your workload a little."

Sims laughed. "Hey, I like that idea. Call me sometime and let me know how you're doing. Or if you need help."

"You've got it, Sims. And thanks for helping resolve this situation."

Rob hung up the receiver with a sigh of satisfaction. He couldn't wait to tell Jessica that Cattaloni was skipping town. If anyone asked him, he'd bet the man wouldn't even contact Jessica's father about the money he owed him.

After all, a million wasn't much to a man like Cattaloni.

In Rob's mind, the man had lost a great deal more when Jessica had walked away. And Rob wasn't going to be so stupid. He and Jessica belonged together.

He checked his watch as he rushed back up to the hotel room. He hadn't intended to be gone so long. It was almost noon. Rapping on the door, he waited for her to open up.

When there was no response, he pulled out the

extra key. He hadn't wanted to barge in, in case she was feeling shy after their lovemaking.

The pristine tidiness of the room chilled him. The bed was made and nothing was out of place. He opened the closet door and was relieved to see their belongings neatly stacked in the closet. She hadn't checked out, at least. But where was she?

He grabbed the phone and called Mrs. Hutchins. "Have you heard from Jessica?"

"Why, no. I thought she was with you."

"I seem to have lost her," he said grimly.

"Mercy. I won't tell the kids. But you'd better find her before you come home."

JESSICA DIDN'T RETURN to the hotel until after five o'clock. Tired and hungry, she leaned against the side of the elevator, deciding to order room service rather than go out on her own.

Memories of dinners prepared by Mrs. Hutchins made her homesick for a home she hadn't known for long. But she'd best forget such silliness.

At least her day had been well spent. The family lawyer had explained several technicalities to her, relieving her mind of some financial difficulties. She could manage quite well until she found a new job and a place to live.

Even better, her father had arrived at the attorney's office while she was there. They hadn't had a grand reunion. Her father wouldn't change overnight. But he'd treated her with respect. And he admitted he'd made a mistake taking money from Stephen.

It was a start.

She'd even looked at a couple of apartments, but nothing tempted her. Her mind skittered away from that word. There was only one person who came to mind with the thought of temptation.

Fortunately the elevator doors slid open and she stepped into the hallway. Her room was nearby. Maybe she should check out of the hotel and find another one. Or even change rooms. One where she hadn't made love with Rob.

When she opened the door, she could still smell his after-shave. This would never do. She decided to call the front desk and crossed to the phone.

Only to find Rob stretched out on the bed.

She gasped and tried to retreat.

He jackknifed up from the bed and grabbed her arm, holding her in place. "Where have you been?"

Before she could even consider answering, he wrapped his arms around her. His lips met hers in a deep kiss, reminiscent of their nighttime activities.

"What are you doing here?" she asked as he raised his head. "Why did you come back?"

He frowned. "You thought I'd just leave, without saying anything?"

"You were gone when I woke up."

"I went downstairs to call about Cattaloni. Didn't you notice my bag was still here?"

"Yes, but— I assumed— I'll get it for you." She pushed away from him.

He wouldn't let her go. "What's wrong with you? I don't care about the bag."

"Then why are you here?"

Now he was the one without words. Finally he gave her a small shake. "Where else would I be? Don't you know that we belong together? Didn't last night prove that to you?"

"I didn't know how you felt. You didn't leave a note. I assumed it didn't— I assumed you wanted sex."

That grin of his that drove her crazy settled once again on his lips. "Hell, yes, I wanted sex. But only with you, sweetheart. For the rest of my life."

As much as her heart leaped at his words, she couldn't allow herself to believe him. "I don't need rescuing again, Rob. Sacrifice isn't necessary."

"Good. Because I'm feeling pretty selfish today." He kissed her neck. "And last night, too."

"What do you mean?"

"I mean I think *you* may have to rescue *me,* Goldilocks. I was so overcome with desire last night, I didn't tell you why I wanted to stay with you, or what I had in mind for our future, if you agree. I think I reacted more like one of those bears, chasing you. Will you forgive me?"

"I—I don't know what you mean."

"I'll try to make up for lost time. I fell in love with you, Goldilocks, long before I knew it. I've been wanting to make love to you since I saw you naked in my bed."

"That's sex, lust."

"You bet it is!" he agreed with a grin. "But I also wanted to protect you, take care of you, keep you with me always." Another kiss. "Is that lust?"

"You like to rescue people."

"It has its moments," he agreed and claimed her lips again, this time for a mind-blowing kiss. When he raised his head, he said, "By the way, Cattaloni is leaving Kansas City. I called Sims after we got to town and he's been checking on your friend Stephen. Your father wasn't his only interest. And some of those deals were already questionable. With a nudge from Sims, Cattaloni has decided the Bahamas would be a better environment for him."

"He's leaving?" Hope flared in Jessica. "You found that out for sure?"

"That's what I was doing this morning. I didn't want to call from here in case I awakened you."

She rested her head on his shoulder, pleased with his information, and yet strangely bereft that Rob wouldn't need to guard her as he had. She decided it would be wise to rule out his other excuse for wanting her.

"But Cathy and Michael already have a mother."

Her non sequitur seemed to startle Rob. "You don't like my kids?"

"I love them!" she returned fiercely. "But—but I wouldn't marry any man just to be with his children."

"Good."

She suddenly realized he'd never used the word marriage. Hastily she tried to rectify her mistake. "Not that anyone has mentioned marriage. I didn't mean—"

"But I should've. I should've told you last night that if you slept with me, you'd be stuck with me for life. Because I can't let you go now, sweetheart.

Unlike the three bears, I'm never going to let you get away."

"People will say I'm marrying you for your money. I'm not rich anymore, remember?"

"I remember. Are you marrying me for my money?"

"No! Love is a lot more important than money."

"And do you love me?"

"Oh, yes," she said with a sigh.

"Then there's no problem. Because I love you with all my heart."

She melted against him, wonder in her eyes. "Really? Are you sure, Rob? It's only been five days. You might change your mind."

"And lose the best accountant I could find? Don't be silly."

"What are you talking about?"

"I told you I had a job for you. I'm starting a security firm. I want to hire you to be my controller."

"Your controller?"

"If you want to. But that position is optional. The position of wife isn't. On that I'm not giving you a choice."

Bossy to the end, Jessica thought, her heart filling with love. But she knew she really had a choice. His gentleness and caring proved that.

"Okay," she agreed, and wrapped her arms around his neck.

"Good." He let out a sigh of relief. "I want you back in Papa Bear's bed...for the rest of our lives."

Goldilocks had no problem with that fairy-tale ending.

Epilogue

"Jessica!" Mrs. Hutchins called up the stairs.

"Yes, Mrs. Hutchins?" she returned, hurrying to the head of the stairs.

"Rob called. He's on his way."

"Good. Where are the kids?"

"Cathy and Goldilocks are in her room. Michael and his dog are in the garage with Mr. H."

Jessica came down the stairs, anxious to meet Rob at the door. "Are you sure you can manage for three days without us?"

"Of course. You two deserve a little time to yourselves. Not too many people take their children on their honeymoon."

"But it was Christmas. We couldn't go off and leave them alone for our first Christmas."

Mrs. Hutchins smiled. "Well, Valentine's Day doesn't have to be shared with children. But I am worried about you getting snowed in."

"Even if we do, I bet you've packed enough food to last us until the spring thaw," Jessica teased. The past three months she'd discovered how caring the woman could be.

Her cheeks flushed, Mrs. H. nodded. "Better safe than sorry. Besides, I don't want you to work. You've been looking a little pale to me lately. I think Rob's asking you to work too much."

Jessica grinned. "He is definitely a slave driver!" When Mrs. Hutchins frowned, Jessica corrected her statement. "I'm just teasing. I've really put in very few hours. And I've enjoyed the work."

The front door opened and Jessica flew past Mrs. Hutchins into her husband's arms.

"Miss me?"

"Every minute," she assured him.

"Ready to go?"

"Um, I need to talk to you, first."

She smoothed away his quick frown with her fingers.

Keeping his arm around her, he led her into the library, her favorite room in their new home. "Is something wrong? Did the kids misbehave?"

"Of course not!" she said indignantly, until she remembered an earlier crisis. "Unless you mean Michael allowing Bear to chew a hole in his newest sweater. But both of them were very sorry."

"Yeah, I bet," Rob said with a grin. He kissed her but a frown returned to his forehead. "Then what's wrong? Don't you want to go back to the cabin?"

"I can't wait. But I thought I should tell you something first. We might want to share it with the rest of the family before we go away."

"What?"

She ducked her head and adjusted his collar. They

hadn't discussed this possibility, and she was nervous about breaking the news to him. "Um, well—"

"You're making me very nervous. Are you telling me you spent all my money and we're flat broke?"

"No."

"Come on, sweetheart, out with it."

"We're going to have another addition to the family."

"Your father's moving in?"

Jessica shook her head. She'd made an improvement in the relationship with her father, but she didn't think they were that close yet. Though she thought he'd like her news.

"You bought another dog? Come on, Jess, two puppies at once is enough."

"Not puppies."

She peeped up at his sudden stillness and was relieved to see joy breaking across his face.

"A baby?" he asked, softly, reverently, pulling back so he could see her face. "We're going to have a baby?"

She nodded and then clutched his neck as he picked her up and swung her around.

"Have you told the others?" he asked as he set her down.

"Of course not. Not before I told you. I wasn't sure— We haven't talked about—"

He kissed her before saying, "I hope you're happy about it, because I'm thrilled. I wasn't around much for Cathy and Michael's early years. Now I feel like I'm being given a second chance."

"Shall we tell them before we go?"

"I think we should. It'll give them a lot to think about while we're gone."

They stepped back into the entryway and called their family together. Cathy came down the stairs with Goldie, as she called her puppy, tucked under her arm. Mr. Hutchins and Michael, with Bear scampering behind, arrived just as Mrs. Hutchins reappeared from the kitchen.

Jessica looked at her family, a family who loved and cared about each other, and couldn't imagine a luckier child than the one she was carrying. And one more to love would only make her true family even better.

HARLEQUIN®
AMERICAN ◆ ROMANCE®

COMING NEXT MONTH

**Next month, celebrate Christmas with American Romance
as we take you
HOME FOR THE HOLIDAYS**

#705 CHRISTMAS IN THE COUNTRY by Muriel Jensen
Now that he was free, ex-hostage Jeff James wanted nothing more than to eat Liza deLane's glazed ham for Christmas. But for the woman touted as the "new Martha Stewart," the *timing* couldn't be worse. She had a borrowed husband, rented kids...and a very big problem!

#706 MARLEY AND HER SCROOGE by Emily Dalton
When Carl Merrick fell asleep at his desk on Christmas Eve, his business partner Marley Jacobs made an unexpected appearance in his dreams. Dressed in a baby-doll nightie, she warned him to change his Scroogelike ways by the stroke of midnight or someone else would be sharing her Christmas future.

#707 BELLS, RINGS & ANGELS' WINGS by Linda Randall Wisdom
One minute Libby Barnes idly wished she didn't have to spend Christmas with her family; the next she wished she'd kept her mouth shut. Because there was her house, there were her parents, there was her husband Ty— but nobody knew who *she* was....

#708 THE SANTA SUIT by Karen Toller Whittenburg
Single mom Kate Harmon had always told her twins the truth— Santa Claus didn't exist. So why had they hired detective Gabe Housley to find him? And why was Kate hoping that Gabe was Santa's answer to the twins' request for a daddy?

AVAILABLE THIS MONTH:

#701 IN PAPA BEAR'S BED
Judy Christenberry

#703 OVERNIGHT WIFE
Mollie Molay

#702 A DARK & STORMY NIGHT
Anne Stuart

#704 MISTER CHRISTMAS
Linda Cajio

Look us up on-line at: http://www.romance.net

Look what Santa brought!

CHRISTMAS DELIVERY

Capture the holiday spirit with these three
heartwarming stories of moms, dads,
babies and mistletoe. *Christmas Delivery*
is the perfect stocking stuffer featuring three
of your favorite authors:

A CHRISTMAS MARRIAGE by Dallas Schulze
DEAR SANTA by Margaret St. George
THREE WAIFS AND A DADDY by Margot Dalton

**There's always room for one more—
especially at Christmas!**

Available wherever Harlequin and Silhouette
books are sold.

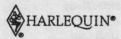

HARLEQUIN®   Silhouette®

Free Gift Offer

With a Free Gift proof-of-purchase
from any Harlequin® book, you can receive
a beautiful cubic zirconia pendant.

This stunning marquise-shaped stone is a genuine cubic
zirconia—accented by an 18" gold tone necklace.
(Approximate retail value $19.95)

Send for yours today...
compliments of ❖HARLEQUIN®

To receive your free gift, a cubic zirconia pendant, send us one original proof-of-purchase, photocopies not accepted, from the back of any Harlequin Romance®, Harlequin Presents®, Harlequin Temptation®, Harlequin Superromance®, Harlequin Intrigue®, Harlequin American Romance®, or Harlequin Historicals® title available at your favorite retail outlet, together with the Free Gift Certificate, plus a check or money order for $1.65 U.S./$2.15 CAN. (do not send cash) to cover postage and handling, payable to Harlequin Free Gift Offer. We will send you the specified gift. Allow 6 to 8 weeks for delivery. Offer good until December 31, 1997, or while quantities last. Offer valid in the U.S. and Canada only.

Free Gift Certificate

Name: _____

Address: _____

City: _____ State/Province: _____ Zip/Postal Code: _____

Mail this certificate, one proof-of-purchase and a check or money order for postage and handling to: HARLEQUIN FREE GIFT OFFER 1997. In the U.S.: 3010 Walden Avenue, P.O. Box 9071, Buffalo NY 14269-9057. In Canada: P.O. Box 604, Fort Erie, Ontario L2Z 5X3.

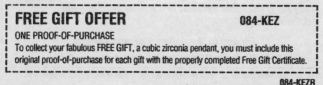

FREE GIFT OFFER
084-KEZ

ONE PROOF-OF-PURCHASE
To collect your fabulous FREE GIFT, a cubic zirconia pendant, you must include this
original proof-of-purchase for each gift with the properly completed Free Gift Certificate.

084-KEZR

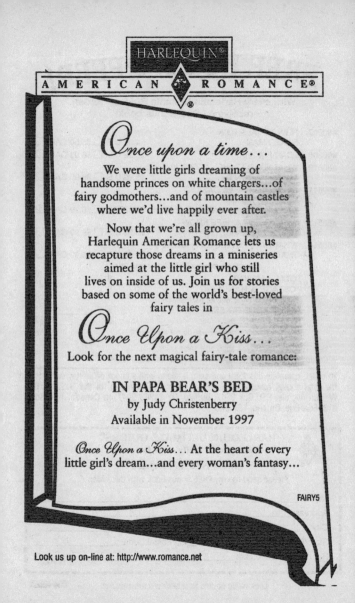

HARLEQUIN®

AMERICAN ❖ ROMANCE®

Once upon a time...

We were little girls dreaming of
handsome princes on white chargers...of
fairy godmothers...and of mountain castles
where we'd live happily ever after.

Now that we're all grown up,
Harlequin American Romance lets us
recapture those dreams in a miniseries
aimed at the little girl who still
lives on inside of us. Join us for stories
based on some of the world's best-loved
fairy tales in

Once Upon a Kiss...

Look for the next magical fairy-tale romance:

IN PAPA BEAR'S BED

by Judy Christenberry
Available in November 1997

Once Upon a Kiss... At the heart of every
little girl's dream...and every woman's fantasy...

FAIRY5